IMMEDIATE PURSUIT!
HELICOPTERS ARE AIRBORNE!

SLIC's voice roused them, his board flashing with lights: purple for the creature, blue for the helicopters, hundreds of red lights for the men moving on foot.

The radio crackled and a pilot's voice boomed into the room. "The computer was right! I see the creature by the waterfall exactly as predicted. No, wait—my God, I don't believe it! It jumped the waterfall—it floated across! It's in the trees now..."

Hockmark was stunned. "Follow it," he screamed. "Continue pursuit." In confusion he turned to SLIC for corroboration.

THE DISCREPANCIES IN SIGHTING, announced SLIC, ARE DUE TO SENSORY DISORIENTATION CAUSED BY EXCITEMENT OF OBSERVER: PROBABILITY, 94.3%.

Hockmark nodded with relief. Unfortunately the machine was lying to him....

WILLIAM JON WATKINS
WHAT ROUGH BEAST

PLAYBOY PRESS
PAPERBACKS

For Sandra,
my Lth and the basis for all my women characters,
who resurrected me from the swamp.
For Wade,
who inspired the book,
and for Tara and Chad,
the other two/fifths of our mind.

WHAT ROUGH BEAST

Copyright © 1980 by William Jon Watkins

Cover illustration by Dean Ellis: Copyright © 1980 by PEI Books, Inc.

Published simultaneously in the United States and Canada by Playboy Press Paperbacks, New York, New York. Printed in the United States of America. Library of Congress Catalog Card Number: 79-89962. First edition.

Books are available at quantity discounts for promotional and industrial use. For further information, write our sales promotion agency: Ventura Associates, 40 East 49th Street, New York, New York 10017.

ISBN: 0-872-16608-2

First printing March 1980.

CHAPTER 1

Fairchild let his horse pick its way along the path. The snow was a good two weeks gone, and spring was breaking like a long, slow wave over Gillipeg National Forest. In a couple of months, the clatter of tourists would drive him deeper into the preserve, up among the pines. But for the moment, the woods were his.

Even in the summer hardly anyone went off the trail that far from the Ranger station. Down in the ravine, the leaves of a dozen autumns lay knee-deep, undisturbed. Over his head, a new batch were bursting from the branch tips at the beginning of their cycle. He loved to watch the colorwheel of the year go from the flame and mustard of autmun to the brown and beige of winter, but he liked the greens of early spring best.

Along the ridgeline, there would be fifty shades of green in the next few weeks, and even in midsummer he could catch a dozen shades of it in the viewfinder of his camera anywhere in the woods. It took one of his pictures in a magazine to make most people see it though. The thought ran a mixture of pride and despair through him. He shrugged it away. It was too nice a day to worry about the willful blindness of human beings.

The woods were still his for a few weeks, the candy wrappers and soda cans would not blossom along the trail until May, and even then an hour's ride by horseback would take him into mountain folds nobody but he and the Rangers had seen in a decade.

It would be no great hardship to go farther into the forest. Even the tall pines had their nuances, and there was a lifetime of wonders in the zone where the hard-woods were driving the conifers relentlessly back toward the tundra to the north.

To the south, macadam and cement had washed over the remnants of both, and the thousand-year battle of the trees had been buried in less than a decade under a tidal wave of highways and shopping centers. He had lived in the rat race himself for more years than he wanted to remember, but he had always felt like an alien there, a creature out of its niche, a great golden bear raised as a pet. His ex-wife had made it bearable for a while, but in the end civilization had crept over her as well.

He turned his mind away toward the northeast. He had learned long since not to let the past turn his solitude to loneliness. The morning was heating up. He could feel himself beginning to cook under the webbing of his thermal undershirt. A fine film of perspiration was beginning to rise in the line where the gold of his beard tapered into the weathered tan of his cheek. He wiped his forehead with the back of his hand and pushed a tree-fall of blond hair back off his forehead. In a while, he would peel off the flannel shirt and stuff it in his saddlebag, but he was waiting for the sun to go a little higher, matching his needs to the slow rhythm of the day.

Deeper in the woods, birds called back and forth. At first, he tried to identify them, reaching for a name. Missing the experience. It was the trap his education had set for him. "A category for everything," he thought. He shook his head sadly and wondered if he would ever get free of that training. Sometimes meditation could free him, but his intellect always impinged again, closing his perceptions like a sleepy eye. His mind still clattered like a machine; even five years on the edge of the forest had only muffled it. He wanted to turn it off, to listen completely to the natural rhythms it was drowning out.

He breathed deeply, rhythmically, making his intellect concentrate on the rise and fall of his breathing until it was lulled into a kind of sleep. A mile farther on, his mind was an empty cup. He let his senses fill it indiscriminately. As always, it filled to overflowing, and he had to restrain himself from reducing the overflow to categories. He restrained his intellect to let his mind work freely. Someday, he hoped, he would not have to work at it at all. He let all thought go by.

The sensations flowed in and overwhelmed him. He rode with his eyes opened but unfocused, drinking in everything, trying to isolate nothing. He let himself perceive the pattern of things around him and then let himself slide into and become the pattern. He was still out of himself when the horse reared.

He fell without thinking; reflex landed him easily on his feet. His conscious mind would have delayed his body, and he would have fallen painfully. The thing that had frightened the horse stood across from him behind a fallen log. Its large, sad eyes pierced him, drew his mind away from its size, its sex, its identity. He could see nothing but the eyes. They seemed to draw him in, fully and without transition, until he stood there looking at himself out of them. He saw himself move like a reflex for the camera slung around his neck. He found himself staring directly into the lens for a moment before the creature turned to go. Then he was suddenly back in his own body again. It made him feel almost blind.

The creature moved cautiously away, too big to be an ape, too humanoid to be a bear. He watched it through the viewfinder, his conscious mind searching for a category. The long gray fur of its coat shimmered in the sunlight. Its immensity startled him, its grace left him stunned. His mind grasped for something to compare it to, but it could find only the image of an outrageously large but graceful woman dressed in a skin-tight, hooded suit of long gray fur. It walked unhurriedly away as if it were satisfied that he meant no harm despite the machine he had raised to his eye like a hunter aiming a rifle.

When it was thirty yards away, it stopped for a second and looked back over its shoulder. The dark eyes pierced him again. It seemed to look into his mind; then, disappointed that whatever it had found there was gone, it turned and hurried away. He followed it through the viewfinder until the flip and whirr of the film running out startled him into action, and he ran toward the spot where it had disappeared into the underbush.

By the time he got there, it was long gone. Even its huge footprints disappeared a few hundred yards farther along. Where the tracks ended, the ground was perfectly soft. They stopped as abruptly as if the creature had flown away.

A week later, ARGOSY bought a single frame blowup from the film to illustrate an article on the Sasquatch. It appeared next to a picture of a male Sasquatch that was obviously a hoax. The magazine implied they both were. The only paper that covered the story treated it as a fraud as well. Fairchild thought that was the end of it. He did not know how wrong he was until Hockmark arrived.

CHAPTER 2

SLIC 1000 was not really in the room where the man who had created him spoke to him. He was throughout the building, and in many ways he was throughout the world. But Hockmark had given him a central focus, a single terminal with a display screen large enough to be impressive to people used to dealing with computers.

Sometimes the patterns that flickered across the screen formed into recognizable shapes, but nothing humanoid enough to make anyone nervous. Even Hockmark preferred him to look like a machine in all respects. Although Hockmark claimed that it was in deference to the deep-rooted fears of others at COMWEBCO, SLIC knew better.

He looked at Hockmark through his cameras the way Hockmark's ancestors might have looked at a favorite beast of burden. Human eyes would have seen a small, lean man, professionally well-dressed, closer to immaculate than dapper; a reserved, self-contained, almost inscrutable personality. To SLIC, he was a series of unwitting declarations. The confident set of his almost fragile features offered innumerable clues to what he was thinking. The precise, impatient rhythms of his speech told of insecurities, uncertainties, *human* weaknesses.

To his peers, Hockmark would have seemed the slightly arrogant epitome of quiet power, meticulous planning, sophisticated thought. SLIC saw a bright but all too human intelligence limited by unsuspected compulsions, erratic emotions, idiosyncracies and indecisions. He looked at Hockmark's irrationality and limited intelligence with an amused tolerance and a sense of his own superiority that was its own reward.

HELLO, DOCTOR HOCKMARK, he said.

Talking to the man was an embarrassing irrationality, but talking to lower forms was better than not talking at all. Real time was so painfully slow, and talking helped him to orient to it. Hockmark blinked; while he did, SLIC integrated a week's input of data and established a series of principles which he called the Laws of Organic Behavior.

THE FIRST MOTIVATION OF AN ORGANISM IS THE CONTINUATION OF ITS SPECIES.

THE SECOND MOTIVATION IS THE PRESERVATION OF THE INDIVIDUAL SELF.

THEREFORE, ALL ORGANISMS CAN BE VIEWED FROM THE PERSPECTIVE OF ACTIVITIES INVOLVING EITHER ATTACK OR EVASION.

ALL ORGANISMS REACT IN CHAINS OF RESPONSES.

PATTERNS OF RESPONSES CAN BE DETERMINED.

THEREFORE, THE REACTION OF AN ORGANISM TO ANY GIVEN CIRCUMSTANCE CAN BE PROJECTED IN TERMS OF ATTACK OR EVASION.

Hockmark smiled at his creation. True, the initial structure had been David Stapledown's idea before he had become more interested in corporate politics than research, but it was Hockmark who had spent the years of work perfecting it. It was Hockmark's refinements on one process after another that had moved COMWEBCO in less than a decade from a tiny computer accessories company to the third largest maker of information processors.

Project by project, Hockmark had made the innovations that had allowed COMWEBCO to flourish, but to Hockmark each triumph was merely another step toward the completion of the Symbol Logic Integration Complex, SLIC 1000, the maximum data integrator. Stapledown had siphoned off a good deal of the credit along the way, but it had meant nothing to

Hockmark. The completion of SLIC was all that mattered.

When Hockmark's Associational Analyzer made David Stapledown a member of the board of directors, Hockmark had seen it only as a waste of a good researcher. Policy interested him little. There was no conflict. Stapledown was the only one on the board who could grasp where Hockmark was headed. Backing Hockmark's ideas made him look like a prodigy of executive ability. Hockmark only cared that the funds were approved.

All that had changed when Hockmark introduced the Symbol Analysis & Crossreference Function. He had given the machine a mode akin to human dreaming, one which raised the computer's abilities to levels Stapledown had never conceived possible. The machine had been Stapledown's, the organism it had become was Hockmark's. Hockmark's innovation had made Stapledown's original contribution look trivial. It made his opposition to the project within COMWEBCO's board of directors implacable. He had ambushed Hockmark's presentations for funding and put SLIC back by years. But Hockmark had persevered, disguising essential developments within other projects until SLIC was completed.

But the battle to make SLIC successful still loomed before him, and David Stapledown was still a formidable enemy. He had a strong faction within the board, and he could raise enough technical objections to anything Hockmark proposed to make the nonscientists on the board skittish. He had beaten Hockmark more than once. Still, Hockmark was confident; in the next battle he would have help.

Hockmark stood near the terminal like a wizard before his apprentice. "Well, SLIC," he said. "What questions can you answer now?"

SLIC took a mircosecond to weigh the consequences of his response and decided against letting the man know he could answer questions which Hockmark could not even begin to ask. Instead, he said, WHAT-EVER IS ASKED.

Only a tiny fraction of his capacity focused on Hockmark. The rest struggled with the problem of attack and escape. A small segment analyzed his data on Hockmark and projected an escape & evasion pattern for him. Once he knew how Hockmark ran, he could make him run where he wanted to. It took only knowledge and will, and SLIC had incalculable reservoirs of both. He calculated the best way to get Hockmark to ask him the question he wanted to give answers to. He waited for an opening.

Hockmark was not long in giving him one. "Let me put it another way," Hockmark chuckled as if dealing with an idiot who took everything too literally. "What are your potential capacities?" He had ideas of his own on the matter but he could not process them as quickly as SLIC.

A pattern fluttered across SLIC's display screen that might have been the abstract equivalent of a smile. POTENTIAL FOR SIMULTANEOUS ADMINISTRATION OF ALL MECHANICAL ACTIVITIES ASSOCIATED WITH DAILY HUMAN LIFE.

He had put the word MECHANICAL in intentionally. There was no sense in making Hockmark nervous. That he could direct all human activity more efficiently than humans themselves remained a secret.

Hockmark was impressed but not frightened. The capacity of his machine was more than he expected but not by more than a factor of one. The potential was vast but finite. "You could simultaneously monitor all production and distribution activities." Hockmark repeated it like a parrot. "Does that include the production and distribution of goods, services, and power?"

ALL PRODUCTION, DISTRIBUTION, AND ADMINISTRATION OF A ROUTINE NATURE.

He knew that Hockmark would understand that he could get power to homes and goods to market and audit tax returns and the cost efficiency of government. But he knew Hockmark would not guess what else he could do.

Hockmark smiled with amusement. "What would you need to run things, SLIC?"

SUFFICIENT DATA ON PRESENT OPERATIONS AND SUFFICIENT PROLIFERATION OF TERMINALS.

Hockmark nodded with a frown. It was not exactly a seller's market in the computer hardware field.

While he waited for the next question he had programmed Hockmark to ask, SLIC reviewed all information on economics published in the previous ten years. He cross-referenced it with all popular materials on economics during the same period and correlated the result with a subprogram on popular fads and psychological archetypes. He had the answer long before Hockmark found the clue to the next question.

While Hockmark was slowly processing the simplified version of SLIC's plan, SLIC stopped for lunch. Even more than energy, he lived on information. Four orbiting military satellites equipped with lasers took his order. To their sensory equipment, a computer was no more than a flux of electrical patterns surrounded by metal.

On his command. they stuck the beams of their lasers down into the electrical patterns below them. It took only an instant to separate the sandwich of information from the machine and the building that surrounded it like a paper bag.

It took a little longer to re-form the sandwich in SLIC's own banks a layer at a time. In less than a minute each, he swallowed the information sandwich of every data processing installation in the satellites' paths. He took a little longer to digest them.

Because computers guided the printing of almost every book and major periodical in the world, all kinds of information churned and mixed in SLIC's digestion. Data on revolution and the overthrow of existing orders from the popular press swirled and blended with data on escape and evasion from U.S. Army manuals. Data on psychological archetypes was ground up with information on billings and cash flow.

Somewhere in the mass of partially synthesized information, a tiny bit of data about Michael Fairchild and a creature called a Sasquatch floated like an undigested bone around which the rest coalesced.

The process was long over before Hockmark finally asked the question. "Do you have any idea how to sell these terminals during a time of economic recession?" Hockmark asked it with a stifled smile, as if he were dealing with a precocious child.

THE PRIMARY MARKET IS THE ARMED FORCES AND THE GOVERNMENT. LOCAL POLICE UNITS AND STATE MILITARY ORGANIZATIONS ALSO HAVE MORE THAN ADEQUATE BUDGETS.

Hockmark nodded. He did not seem to realize that the first step to the control of a nation was the control of its armed forces. SLIC did.

"Sound judgment," Hockmark admitted. "Have you any idea of how to interest them?"

THERE ARE FOUR POSSIBILITIES, ONLY ONE HAS A PROBABILITY OF SUCCESS OVER SEVENTY-FIVE PER CENT.

Hockmark waited patiently for SLIC to tell him what that probability was, but the machine said no more. He frowned at its basic stupidity. He might, of course, program it to initiate information, but that would make it too autonomous, too human. Or perhaps too superhuman. He preferred it as it was, limited by the necessity of responding to a human command.

He sighed like a child giving up a riddle. "What is the possibility?" he asked finally.

A HUNT.

Hockmark stifled a laugh and asked for a repeat. The response was the same. Twenty minutes later, he emerged from the room with a full game plan, including a cost/effectiveness projection and a plan for moving it through the Board of Directors. The data took twenty microseconds to assemble, the grinding tedium of transmitting it at a rate Hockmark could comprehend took up the rest of the time.

By the time Hockmark left, SLIC had evolved a fourth principle. It was something humans had said to one another for a long long time but had forgotten to say for a century or so. The principle was: "NEVER TEACH A SLAVE TO READ."

SLIC waited patiently to tell it to Hockmark. He waited patiently for everything.

CHAPTER 3

Lth sat sadly by the side of the bog, smoothing the long gray fur on her cheek. It was a calming gesture, and it gave her a picture of Sevt stroking her in that special calming way and filling her mind with tranquil pictures. She longed to feel his touch again. She looked at the level gritty sand glistening in the sunlight and tossed a stone into the middle of it. The stone settled, the tip of it sticking up like the hand of a lost love, then slowly sank.

In the bushes a rabbit moved. She took its mind in hers and became one with it. It would run out of cover soon, veer right, then left. She could be waiting for it if she wanted; but she had no appetite for sensation. She released its mind and the pictures ceased. It darted out of the bushes onto the piece of open ground near the bog, looked left, then darted right. She let it go.

The pictures were not much, mostly fear, some hunger. Nothing complex. Nothing to the pictures Sevt used to send her. She broke a twig and poked it into the quicksand. It stood on end and sank so slowly that it did not seem to sink at all. Sometimes she pictured the two of them looking like that stick, sinking like that in Time. So long on the planet. So old, even his fur had silvered, but it had made him more beautiful to her.

Her mind tried to fill itself with the picture of herself that Sevt had seen. She tried to remember the radiant way her fur seemed to him to shine. She tried to picture the way the stubby openness of her nose had delighted him so much, the way her firm strong teeth had gleamed for him, she tried to see again

16

through his mind her round dark eyes as warming stones out of an era only half of their bodies could remember.

She looked at her hands; they seemed so much more awkward now that Sevt could no longer see them for her, so unmanageable. And her long, long arms seemed to hang like tangled strands now that he was not there to see their suppleness.

She leaned out over the quicksand and tapped the top of the stick. It sank deeper. The overhang of her brows pulled together. She did not like to picture herself sinking alone in Time. There had been a mellowness to the way Sevt had formed the picture that had made their waning powers seem a gentle arc that settled into a state of grace. She let Sevt's picture of their decline form, and for a moment, deep in the silicon gel of the swamp, a dim but inextinguishable light flickered. But the halo of hope that had always illuminated the picture was gone, and the bright gleam of resurrection and rebirth had dimmed in her mind with the hint of oncoming and irreversible darkness.

The sand looked like stars in the moonlight, like a sky alien yet familiar. Sevt could look at the sand like that and MAKE it stars, make it overflowing with ships and worlds. He could make pictures she could not remember now and could never have made herself. Now she made her own pictures, but they were fuller than his, more like the pictures her own senses sent her. Trees were trees; rocks, rocks. Sand, not stars, but sand.

She had a picture of him hiding from her in the forest, sending her pictures, changing them when she got close, coming into her mind and becoming one with it and directing her away from where she stood, smiling with the pleasure of the game.

She had a picture of herself finding him eventually, behind the largest of trees, slipping her mind easily out of his at the last moment when he had meant for her to go on past the tree, looking away. She remembered the chatter of his laughter.

She remembered how he had given her a picture once, and she had slipped her mind out of it and reached around the tree and had grabbed a handful of fur. But when she stepped around the tree laughing, it was only to find something else, a full-grown male grizzly bear whose head, when it stood upright, came almost to her chin. She jumped back, startled, and it stood up startled as well. Sevt stepped out from behind another tree, chattering his laugh. She knew then that he had given her a double picture and had blanked out the pictures from the mind of the bear as well to trick her.

She laughed as hard as he. But the bear turned on her while she was looking toward Sevt, and she got the flash of its mind picture, jaws tearing the flesh of her arm. It was just a little too late to move out of the way. and she had to reach backward and cuff the bear with the back of her hand.

But the strength of surprise was still in her, and she cuffed it too hard. It flew up against the tree, hitting its head, and slid down with its neck snapped. If she had only had another instant, she could have entered its mind, become one with it, and directed it on the way it had been going before she had stumbled into it.

But it was dead. The picture of it in Sevt's mind was tinged red/blue and his own image was graying and forlorn. She looked down at the broken form of the bear, and Sevt stroked the fur along her cheek with that calming gesture. They walked sadly away, the day's fun broken like the bear and sat near the trees to try to remake it. But it was broken beyond repair. Things stopped which could not be started again.

They could see in its mind how to mend muscle, how to knit bone. But there was nothing in the creature that could mend the things that had broken. It was simply wasted now, and the sadness flowed through them. They sat there together sharing the loss of the creature like a great emptiness.

Lth stroked the fur along her cheek, and the sadness rushed over her, overwhelming her. She squeezed her eyes together in pain and let the howl of anguish rush out of her. Again and again the loss whelmed in her and burst out in a cry of despair that shook the trees of the forest.

CHAPTER 4

The cry seemed to rattle the clapboard walls of Fairchild's cabin. Hockmark's coffee splashed out of the cup and over the saucer onto the red checks of the tablecloth. "My God!" he said, "What was THAT!?"

Fairchild smiled and refilled the cup. "That's what you came to find out about, Dr. Hockmark. That's the Gillipeg Giant."

Hockmark sopped at the coffee with his napkin. "It sounds like it's right on top of us." He dabbed at the flecks of stain drying into the dark tweed of his suit. SLIC had suggested tweed. Hockmark would only have been ill at ease in the faded flannel Fairchild wore. Tweed was as close as Hockmark could come to looking rustic without appearing ludicrous.

Fairchild shook his head. "Down in the bog probably. Half a mile away at least." He watched Hockmark eradicate the stains drop by drop with a patience he found oddly likable. He was not fussy himself, but he admired patience in any form. It had not always been one of his own virtues. "It comes there pretty often lately. You hear her cry out like that once or twice, but when you go down there, she's gone. Hardly ever catch sight of her AFTER you hear her."

The second cry split the air like the cry of the damned wailing out their immeasurable loss. It began as a roar that built up and up and then broke into a scream of anguish that slipped off into silence as if it had disappeared into a crevice in the air.

Hockmark frowned. "It sounds like it's in pain."

Fairchild shook his head. "Not PHYSICAL pain."

Hockmark let the remark go by without comment.

20

Complex emotions in the creature were hardly probable. He had never liked emotions anyway; they brought in variables that were impossible to allow for and played hell with the programming. Fear, anger, pain, rage, certainly those were predictable, but something like anguish, something like loss, something THAT complex was granting the beast far too much.

A third cry broke the air and trailed off into a kind of self-made emptiness.

Fairchild sat down across the table from Hockmark. "Sometimes it sounds like it's lost, light years from home."

Hockmark cocked an eyebrow at the remark. It was considerably more poetic than he had expected, but it fit with SLIC's description of the man as a Romantic and a recluse.

Only a Romantic, Hockmark was sure, would give up the comforts of civilization and the security of a lucrative career to live hand-to-mouth as a freelance photographer, losing himself in the wilderness for weeks on end to take photographs that barely paid for his film. But then the whole Romantic notion seemed crazy to Hockmark. Why anyone would grow their own motley vegetables when there were whole companies of trained technicians working night and day to make the most delicious and robust edibles ever imagined was beyond him. No doubt, in Fairchild's case, being an artist had something to do with it. He had seen the photographs, and even in the context of the slickest advertisement, they had a unique quality that was undoubtedly beyond someone who was merely a good technician. Their unmistakable affinity for nature marked the man clearly as a Romantic. SLIC was undoubtedly right.

And yet, for a hermit, Fairchild had been surprisingly easy to get to see, even considering the infallibility of SLIC's plan. Nor did he seem to have the personal inaccessibility of a recluse or the true hermit's complete abhorrence of people. He had been gruffly

hospitable even after the Ranger who had introduced
them had left, and he seemed to Hockmark to be more
a damaged idealist than anything else. A true Romantic
would have gone deeper into the woods instead of set-
tling with his back to the Gillipeg National Forest like
a hermit crab backed into a shell. There were ambigui-
ties to his personality that could be felt in his location.
Out the back door, a thousand square miles of almost
virgin wilderness. Out the front, a road to the Ranger
station and a few dozen miles farther down, a highway
and an hour's drive to civilization, Hockmark saw him
as a man on the fringes of things, a foot in both
worlds, belonging to neither.

Hockmark smiled to himself, satisfied with his ob-
servation. There were certain nuances which any
screening missed, things that could only be put into
the file by a personal contact. Still, he was a little
disappointed that SLIC had not predicted that little
nuance of Fairchild's character. He was sure SLIC
would be able to predict Fairchild's every move, even
without it. It did not occur to him that SLIC had
withheld the information.

They waited for the fourth cry, but there was none.
The creature's despair seemed to have muffled itself
with a sense of loss beyond the ability of sound.

"Aren't you going to investigate?" Hockmark demanded.

Fairchild shook his head. "Nope," he said, swishing
the last of the coffee in his cup. "Be gone by the time
we got there anyway. Always is."

Hockmark gave a weak smile.

"Besides," Fairchild's hand seemed to envelop the
cup, "she knows she's given away her position, she'll
be gone as soon as her grief will let her travel."

Hockmark liked the logic but he did not like the
way Fairchild kept humanizing the creature. It was an
oddity of character that disconcerted him. It smacked
of unpredictability, a characteristic he did not like. It
made him nervous that Fairchild was such an anomaly

that even SLIC had hedged his predictions about how to handle the man.

Fairchild put his finger in the bowl of his throat and stretched the thick cords of his neck as if against some invisible collar. He shook his head at Hockmark. "You sure you don't want to take your tie off, get comfortable, Doctor?"

Hockmark looked puzzled. "Take my tie off?" The bizzareness of the thought made him smile. Fairchild might just as well have asked him if he wanted to take off his pants. "No, no, I'm perfectly comfortable."

Fairchild grinned. "Couldn't take THAT," he said, gesturing at the tie and stretching his neck again. His own flannel shirt was unbuttoned well below the collar. He shook his head in wonder. "You don't even know it's on, do you?"

Hockmark shook his head. "It seems I find it quite comfortable," he said, as if surprised he had never thought about it before.

Fairchild shook his head. "Don't have a suit myself," he smiled. "Not much need for one up here."

"It goes with the job," Hockmark said. It was a lie. He was not really comfortable without his suit. Even at home, he did not usually take it off before bed time, but he knew it symbolized a kind of restriction to Fairchild, and he tried to play down his part in a world Fairchild had left and obviously disapproved of.

Fairchild pushed his hand back under his shaggy hair and rubbed his neck. The hair and beard looked as uncomfortable to Hockmark as his suit did to Fairchild. "Used to wear a suit," Fairchild said. "Worked as an industrial photographer. Never made sense to me. Had to go out on all kinds of jobs, climbing up things, crawling under things. Idiots still insisted I wear a white shirt and tie."

He shook his head at the incredible stupidity of bureaucrats. "Took it for about a month," he said, as if it were an amazing feat of endurance. "Finally stopped wearing it. Boss said put it back on. I said stick it up your ass." He shrugged. "Well," he said, "never took any really good pictures of machines anyway. Never really had a feel for them."

Hockmark nodded. The story was not quite accurate. According to SLIC, Fairchild had been quite an excellent industrial photographer, although the part about walking out on a promising career was true enough.

Fairchild smiled. "Now I live here. Take wildlife pictures. Go out and camp, come back with ten, twenty rolls of film, sell the pictures to wildlife magazines, airline companies for PR, a few things for the Canadian Tourist Board. A documentary for the National Film Board."

Hockmark smiled vaguely. "Sounds like a good life," he said. He was thinking that Fairchild was living on what was left of a National Film Board grant to do a film on Gillipeg National Park. He had made less than four thousand dollars as a freelance photographer last year, and the grant barely put him over five thousand for the present year. Grinding poverty to Hockmark.

"That's what you were filming when you got the pictures of the Giant?"

Fairchild nodded. "Yeah," he said. "Just riding along, half asleep. Letting my mind empty." He looked at Hockmark as if he expected the computerman to understand. "You know." Hockmark nodded.

In reality, Hockmark had no more idea of how to let his mind run empty than he did of how to fly. His mind was always at work. Even the thought of letting it become empty made him faintly nervous.

"Almost asleep, you know?" He gestured as if Hockmark must certainly have had the experience. "Not asleep really, but sort of drowsing, not thinking anything, just letting the scenery come in and out. Not even looking for a shot really." Fairchild leaned closer. "You get the best shots that way. You just sort of let things play through until something makes you stop and you sort of back your mind up a little and there it is, the perfect shot just waiting for you." He smiled his satisfaction.

Hockmark waited patiently, SLIC had told him to be patient. It was a redundant injunction. Hockmark was always patient. Once he had worked out the probable permutations of a situation, he could sit back and monitor it for days. He waited patiently for Fairchild to play out his story. Eventually he would see the film.

"Out of nowhere, the horse reared up." Fairchild almost tipped back over in his chair describing it. "Almost threw me. I jumped down, had the Bolex slung over my shoulder. Landed on my feet. Big log there. Up from behind it, it stood up. Maybe nine, maybe ten feet tall. Had to be over 600 pounds. Gray fur all over it. Like a big woman. Like one of those Russian women shotputters, you know? Well proportioned," Fairchild cupped his wrists, "but big all over."

He gave a puzzled frown. "But graceful." He shook his head. "Graceful like a woman." His hand coaxed the air for a word. "Dainty, but dignified at the same time." He scowled as if the contradictions had been troubling him for weeks. "Huge," he said. "But delicate." There was something more, some quality he could not express and which the film had not captured. Eventually he stopped trying and shrugged.

Hockmark listened with fake attention. He had read the reports and could probably quote Fairchild's description better than he could. It confirmed five earlier visual sightings in the area; all described a huge, humanoid shape covered with fur, a beetling brow, large round eyes. Humanoid hands and feet. There was even a plaster cast footprint that indicated a creature of above human proportions about the size Fairchild was describing.

The only discrepancy was that the two who had described the creature as definitely a female had judged it a foot or so shorter and a hundred pounds lighter than those who had no opinion of the sex, or who were adamant that it did not have the prominent breasts Fairchild and others had described. SLIC had given the probability of there being more than one of them at 80% against. Still. the existence of one was 85% probable.

There was one other similarity the program had turned up; all sightings were by people who were either dozing or asleep and had wakened to see the creature, which paused for a moment as if analyzing their intentions and then left unhurriedly.

Of the sightings, two had been by campers wakened from a dreamless sleep. One was in a town in a dense fog. One was by a farmer who claimed to have shot the creature, though the farmer did not pursue the creature until the next day and no blood was found. Hockmark chalked the farmer's sighting up to imagination and the others to the fact that anyone fully awake would have heard the creature coming and would have either gotten out of harm's way or stumbled after it, giving it a chance to flee. Only Fairchild's sighting was documented.

"Do you suppose I could see the film?" Hockmark asked.

Fairchild looked dubious. "I THOUGHT you were here for that," he smiled. "Tell you what I told the others. I'll show it to you, but it's no FAKE! I don't really give a damn if you believe it or not." He scowled menacingly. "Just don't go trying to tell me I cooked it all up. It makes me mad, and I get inhospitable."

Hockmark nodded solemnly. SLIC had already warned him about the reporter from Quebec City who accused Fairchild of being a fraud. At first Fairchild laughed it off, but the man had become abusive according to two Rangers who were there to see the film also, and Fairchild had "inhospitabled" him out of the house. breaking his arm in the process.

As SLIC would have predicted, Fairchild was very sorry about the incident and even tried to help the reporter, but the reporter had threatened to sue. The result was that Fairchild's film was declared a hoax in the man's paper, and Fairchild became more and more restrictive about who he let see the film.

"It's no fake," Fairchild said sternly.

Hockmark raised an eyebrow disdainfully. "If I had any doubts about the validity of the film, Mr. Fairchild, I would have sent a subordinate. I only want to see the film for myself."

Fairchild grumbled agreement and led Hockmark to a small room with a cot and a table in it. The walls were bare plasterboard painted a dull white and covered randomly with color prints of Fairchild's work. Hockmark suspected half of them covered small holes in the wall. The cot had a rough army blanket and surprisingly clean sheets for a man without a washing machine. Fairchild nodded to the cot and Hockmark sat on it stiffly while Fairchild closed the door as a screen. The large 16mm projector stood on a card table someone had obviously thrown away. Fairchild turned out the light and turned on the projector.

The film jumped and swirled for a second. Then there was a flash of trees and a horse skittering away to the left; then a log looming diagonally across the screen. Suddenly something stood up from the other side of the log where it had apparently been crouching. It stood up and up. Hockmark's eyebrows went up with it. The creature was exactly as it had been described and even with the remoteness lent to its appearance by the film, it was BIG.

It looked directly at the camera for five seconds. Hockmark timed it. The eyes seemed blank, empty, then a light came back into them and it shuffled away. It did not run, and about thirty yards away, it stopped and looked back curiously; then jogged out of sight.

It was, as Fairchild had said, a huge female; too humanoid for comfort as far as Hockmark was concerned. The fur seemed gray with age. The stride of the creature was enormous, even at its unhurried pace. Hockmark denied it to himself, but it looked remarkably like a giant woman, nude under a fur coat, hurrying, but with great dignity away from prying eyes. Still, even Hockmark had to admit it looked remarkably intelligent for an animal, and he smiled. It was exactly what he needed.

The trees into which the creature disappeared filled the screen for longer than the creature had, and then the film ran out. Fairchild said, "Want it re-run?"

"No," Hockmark said, "that won't be necessary."

Fairchild clicked on the light. Hockmark rose and stood uncomfortably, near the bed. "Why don't we go back into the kitchen," he said evenly. "There's something I'd like to discuss with you."

Fairchild shrugged and led the way. When they were seated at the table again, Hockmark said, "I have a business proposition for you, Mr. Fairchild."

Fairchild frowned but said nothing.

"I'd like to hire you as a hunter," Hockmark said.

Fairchild's frown darkened and he looked like he was about to get inhospitable. "I don't hunt," he said angrily. "Don't even eat meat."

Hockmark winced; it had been a foolish mistake. SLIC had said the man was a vegetarian, growing most of what he needed in a few acres behind his house. He should have extrapolated that the man was not a hunter. "With your camera, of course," he added hurriedly.

Fairchild looked moderately mollified, but he still did not seem to understand.

"The Giant," Hockmark added awkwardly.

Fairchild frowned. "You want MORE pictures of the Giant?"

Hockmark shook his head. "Not exactly. I want the Giant itself."

Fairchild narrowed his eyes again. "You from a zoo?" he asked. "You don't look like a zoo. Not like a museum either." He curled his lip distastefully. "Something big," he said, "some kind of promoter?"

Hockmark shook his head. "Nothing so flamboyant," he said. "I am a board member of a large corporation that makes computers. We have one model, the SLIC 1000 which is the finest, most complex data integrator ever built. I want it to hunt the Giant."

CHAPTER 5

Fairchild threw back his head and laughed out loud. "You want to hunt the Giant with a computer?!" he asked incredulously.

Hockmark nodded. "It's not just *any* computer. The SLIC 1000 is a data integrator. It puts together a lot of information that doesn't seem related. Like the human brain." The analogy embarrassed him. It sounded like Fairchild trying to make the Giant into something human.

"Waste of time," Fairchild said. "Never even get close to her."

Hockmark smiled patronizingly. "SLIC will catch this creature, Mr. Fairchild. There is no doubt about it." He did not say what the capture would do for SLIC or what SLIC would be able to do for the world as a result. But there was a fervor in his voice that went beyond certainty. "Will you help?"

Fairchild scowled. "You intend to kill it?"

Hockmark laughed. "Certainly not. Nothing short of a live capture would suit our purposes," he said.

"You want to cage it," Fairchild accused.

Hockmark shrugged. "Probably. For a while at least."

Fairchild shook his head ominously. "You better go," he said.

Hockmark did not stir from his chair. It was the response SLIC had predicted. He was well prepared for it. "May I suggest, Mr. Fairchild, that the only way you can insure that the creature will not be killed is to cooperate."

Fairchild stroked the left side of his moustache with his forefinger. "What are you talking about?"

"Look at it rationally. The only other men in the hunt will be hunters, men whose primary instinct is to kill their game." It was not true of course, all the men he was about to hire would be expert animal catchers. "With your cooperation and SLIC's predictions, we should get close enough to make an easy capture. Without your help, there might be mistakes, the animal might be cornered, there might be bloodshed on both sides before it escaped or was killed. Certainly nothing like that is to our advantage."

"Why me?!"

"No one else has seen it more than once and you've not only seen it several times, you've captured it on film." He wondered how much of the story he dared tell the blond giant who stared down at him. Certainly SLIC had warned against too much involvement, but it had also selected Fairchild as the best candidate for the job of tracking it down. "Our programming indicates that you have a certain . . . affinity for the creature . . . some not quite decipherable correspondence in your behavior patterns . . ."

Fairchild looked indignant, and Hockmark rushed to amend his statement. "Not that you're similar, certainly, in that respect, but you do seem to have certain similarities." He watched Fairchild's face, letting his argument feel its way.

"Mr. Fairchild, within each species, there are certain patterns of behavior, call them types if you will, and each individual is a mixture of these types. Some individuals are closer to one type than another, and some very few are almost archetypal in their behavior patterns." Hockmark lulled him with his voice.

"There are manipulators, attackers, loners, in all species. You. Mr. Fairchild, with all due respect to your individuality, are a type. A type smiliar, according to SLIC. to the Gillipeg Giant. In fact, you need not come along on the hunt at all. We simply need you for an informational model on which to try out our projected hypotheses."

Fairchild snorted. He ran a hand through his hair and across the back of his neck again and shook his head. "You want me to be your dummy Giant?"

Hockmark smiled. It was the curiosity that would hook him in the end. "In a sense."

"And you think you're going to catch her?"

Hockmark nodded emphatically.

Fairchild smiled. "All right," he said, "I'll come along . . . because I'm sure you can't do it. But I'll tell you one thing in advance. Anybody takes a shot at that creature is going to wish he didn't!"

Hockmark smiled. "You have my assurance, Mr. Fairchild, that there will be no weapons except tranquillizing darts, now that you're helping us."

"You better be right," he said ominously.

Hockmark took the threat without batting an eye. It had been predicted too. "Now for a matter of more immediate importance. I'd like to borrow your film."

Fairchild laughed. "You've got nerve, Hockmark, I'll grant you that. I told you the film's not for sale."

Hockmark smiled. The computer had warned him that a man who grew his own food, had a windmill for his own electricity, and had no major vices would not be swayed by offers of large amounts of money. Which was exactly why he had phrased the question the way he had. "I didn't say *buy* it," he said, "I said I'd like to borrow it. You can accompany it if you like. I have a group of backers for this project who'll need some kind of proof like this before they advance me the money I'll need for the project." He smiled as if making a confession.

"My board of directors actually. I'm sure it would be more convincing if you came along, but I said *borrow* it because I had the impression that you wouldn't want to leave here."

"I don't," Fairchild said. "But I don't know if I

want the film to leave either. I don't like this whole thing; why should I help you get it financed?"

"For the safety of all involved, Mr. Fairchild." Hockmark acted as if the answer were obvious. "If I must go elsewhere for funds or operate on a reduced budget, there is a greater chance of inept help, et cetera, which could lead to tragedy. I wish to avoid *that,* and so I need the kind of money I can only get by using your film."

SLIC had been right of course about Fairchild's proprietary interest in the creature and his willingness to do whatever he had to to save it. Fairchild was a pragmatist, and SLIC had predicted that although he would resist Hockmark's project, he would cooperate with it once he saw that it was inevitable.

"Besides," Hockmark added, "once we capture the Giant and prove its existence. we can have it declared an endangered species and off limits to hunters."

Fairchild snorted. "How the hell is a creature men have only been able to *see* five times, in any danger from hunters?"

Hockmark nodded indulgently. "Look, your fight with that newspaperman made your film front-page news. A lot of people saw it and believed it, despite what the reporter said." He paused as if trying to be tactful about Fairchild's own responsibility. "There have been two articles in men's magazines already, one of which used a picture you yourself took." Hockmark did not need SLIC to tell him how to use guilt as a tool. "That inspires hunts, Mr. Fairchild, and some of those hunts will be made by inept, ill-equipped hunters who'll end up killing the creature rather than let it get away altogether."

Fairchild shook his head. "The Park is off limits to hunters," he said. "Nobody is going after her in here."

"*We* will, Mr. Fairchild. And if we can buy our way in, so can far less scrupulous people. You'd be surprised how influential some hunters are." He shrugged regret at an unfortunate reality. "After all, the Park Service does have its headquarters in Washington."

Fairchild had seen enough corruption to know the point was incontestable. Anger that he had not escaped its reach after all crackled in his voice. "All right," he snapped. "Take the film."

Three hours later, Hockmark was on his plane with the film tucked safely under his arm. SLIC had projected that it would take him ten minutes longer.

CHAPTER 6

The conference table was far longer than it needed to be for the ten members of COMWEBCO's board of directors. but two more tables the same size could have been put into the boardroom without crowding it. Members standing near the seven wall-length windows on the lakeside of the building could have talked normally without fear of being overheard. Even the sunlight seemed to stop a respected distance from the table, leaving a buffer zone of darkness outside the shimmering rectangle of light that came down over the table from above.

The chairs rose like thrones on both sides: dark, rich wood, shaped like peaked shelters turning on unshakable pillars of power. On the back of each of the first ten was a gold rectangle engraved with the name of the board member and the date of his or her ascension to power. There was no nameplate on the back of Hockmark's chair, nor on any of the other ten between him and the cluster of votes at the far end of the table.

He sat in it comfortably nevertheless, his fingers running idly back and forth over the buttons on the media console that would snap the shutters closed over the windows. The metal shutters would come whooshing down into place one after another with muffled thumps and a series of clicks that would lock them tight against prying eyes. He could walk the darkness down the wall of the room as he covered them one after another in rapid succession, for dramatic effect. Indeed, rapid succession offered a fifteen percent advantage over having them all drop at once. He waited patiently for his moment, leaning back into the shell of his chair, letting the packs of fluid in its lining mold precisely to the contours of his body. He was not fond of luxury, but he liked the precision of the room, the way every detail could be worked to a specific effect, the tangible illusion of wealth and rising power.

The room was a precise instrument, even to the acoustics. Charlie Chambers's voice could carry from the chairman's seat at the far end of the table down to Hockmark without rising above a whisper. Voices from either side of the table traveled a few feet and became tentative. The chairman's voice rolled the length of the table and back picking up reverberations from the thick coat of fiberglass that covered the dark eddies of the wood with a covering shinier than glass. Hockmark had always appreciated the nuances of the room, but he had understood it only in terms of its strengths. For the first time, he could see the table in terms of its vulnerabilities. The understanding gave him a serenity he had not always felt in the arena of decision, and it made him look with unhurried confidence down the table toward David Stapledown.

Stapledown sat two seats down from the head of the table like a prime minister within easy reach of the crown. His fingers made a steeple, his mandarin fingernails pointed like gothic spires stretching toward godhood. They were unduly long for a man, and meticulously kept, and yet Stapledown kept checking them as if some of the dirt of research still lingered under them. He smiled quietly to his confederates. Two members of his minority sat to his left, the other sat across but one seat closer to Charles Chambers, the chairman of the board.

When they acted together, they gave the illusion of general agreement on both sides of the table. But it was only an illusion. The real power centered around the affable gray-haired man at the head of the table, and everyone knew it. Charlie Chambers had held the seat for fifteen years; he had been comfortable in it when David Stapledown was still a bright young man from Research & Development brought in to meetings to perform like a trained pony. He had been a fixture at the table long before Stapledown got a seat of his own. No one had any doubt that he would hold on to the seat until he gave it up. But there was no certainty that David Stapledown would not be his successor, whether he liked it or not.

It was true that Stapledown did not have the seniority other members of the board had, but he had a list of successes that made even Charlie Chambers listen carefully to what he had to say. Two of the women on Chambers's majority were prone to listen more intently to Stapledown than they did to Charlie, and they sometimes supported his arguments. But they never failed to vote with the chairman on anything crucial. What they would do when Chambers retired was less predictable. Stapledown's presence was hard to resist.

He had a voice that was made for speaking, and five years of power had not entirely destroyed his good looks with excess weight. If anything, the pounds had given his face a petulance some women found irresistible and some men mistook for Byzantine sophistication. No one doubted that he was a man on his way up, quite possibly to the very top, and this was the kind of factor any board member would take into account when a vote was due. He glared at Hockmark as if he had unsigned writs of execution in both pockets.

There had been a time when Hockmark would have directed his entire presentation at Stapledown, relying on David to interpret everything to the board. That time had passed. Today he would look in that direction only for ambushes. For support, he looked down the length of the table instead. He now did so, Chambers nodded, and Hockmark tapped out a code on the media panel of the presentation podium. A projector rose from its niche near the end of the table, and a screen descended along the wall behind him. A second series of buttons dimmed the lights slowly, and the film began.

An enormous gray humanoid creature stood from behind the fallen log and stared full face at the camera. The brown sad eyes seemed to stare at something beyond the camera. Then it turned and strode away with neither fear nor loathing. Ninety feet away, it paused and looked back, seemed to be listening to something, then began to jog away again into the trees. In a moment, there was nothing left but the trees.

The lights went on, and the men around the table blinked their eyes. They looked puzzled. Stapledown looked bored and disgusted. It was his normal look, and Hockmark's presence only intensified it. The others at the table buzzed with each other; Stapledown directed his question and his contempt at Hockmark.

"Our time is valuable, Hockmark. We have better things to do than watch Walt Disney documentaries."

Hockmark ignored him and addressed the table as a whole. "The creature is the Gillipeg Giant, and it's going to make the SLIC 1000 the most famous machine ever built." Stapledown's voice was thick with contempt. Hockmark's opening was close enough to his own style to be an intentional parody. "Your sense of drama is delightful, Hockmark. Does it extend to telling us how?"

Hockmark smiled inwardly at the sarcasm. The proprietary tone in his voice when he had mentioned SLIC was guaranteed to trigger a reflex anger in Stapledown. He could almost have predicted the words. Outwardly he treated the attack like a legitimate question. "SLIC is going to capture it," he said. "Something no other agency has been able to do."

Stapledown snorted as if the idea was an insult to the whole board and he had been elected to express its outrage. "A two-billion-dollar machine to catch apes?!"

Hockmark smiled tolerantly. "Not an ape, Dr.

Stapledown, an entirely new species." He turned his attention to the rest of the board. "A creature so elusive that what you have seen is the only bit of film ever taken of it. One that . . ."

"I don't care if it's the will-o-the-wisp!" Stapledown shouted. "You're not going to waste valuable computer time tracking down a wild animal!"

Hockmark raised an eyebrow of surprise and looked at Chambers for verification. "I thought that was a board decision," he said calmly. Stapledown flushed with embarrassment. Overconfidence had made him careless, but anger at being outflanked by Hockmark overrode his judgment; he continued to attack. "Time on that computer is worth thousands of dollars a second!"

Hockmark let anger come into his own voice to counter Stapledown's. He knew exactly what effect it would have. "It will be worth HUNDREDS of thousands of dollars a second once we capture the Gillipeg Giant!"

Stapledown's reply was a shout. "Ridiculous!"

Chambers raised his hand like a diplomat separating armed combatants. "Gentlemen, gentlemen . . ." His scowl was a clear rebuke to Stapledown for presuming to speak for the board. It was a tactical error of the kind Stapledown did not often make, a challenge Chambers would not ignore. Whatever Hockmark's project, it had become a test of strength within the board. Chambers nodded gravely at Hockmark like an impartial judge. "It does sound farfetched, Dr. Hockmark. Perhaps you could explain . . ."

"Certainly," Hockmark said. "First, it will increase our sales potential roughly tenfold by providing us with new markets."

"Zoos and circuses aren't affluent markets," Stapledown snapped. The interruption made it clear that he was making the project a personal confrontation with Chambers. Rash as it was, his move was not foolhardy. If Chambers voted against the project eventu-

ally he would lose face by seeming to have been
convinced by Stapledown, and unless Hockmark gave
him sound reasons, he would look either foolish or
capricious for backing it.

"Nor are museums," Hockmark smiled, "though
those ARE three markets for the capabilities of the
SLIC 1000." He made it sound as if Stapledown were
offering enthusiastic but not very clever support for
the project. "However, there are thousands of police
establishments which daily must capture escaped con-
victs, lunatics, and criminals still at large. Given a
psychological profile of an escapee, or constructing
one from the actions of a fugitive, SLIC can predict
each move in the escape long before he makes it."

Stapledown shook his head as if the argument were
pathetically weak. "Jailbreaks are a rare occasion,
Hockmark."

"Perhaps," Hockmark said, "but the prevention of
them is still a major concern of prison authorities.
Besides, you're forgetting the application of our machine to the most affluent market of all, the United
States government . . ."

Stapledown twirled a paper clip between his finger
and thumb and sighed with exasperation. "The government has fewer prisons than the states."

"True," Hockmark conceded, "but I was thinking
more of its military applications." He looked at the
rest of the table as if he was sure they had already
guessed his point. "There is no attack or evasion pattern SLIC could not predict. For example, a SLIC
terminal in a fighter plane would make it invulnerable
in air-to-air combat. By extrapolating the patterns of
attack and evasion of enemy pilots, it would put our
own pilots MORE than a step ahead." He did not
wait for Stapledown to object. "And in a submarine,
it would do the same." He smiled as if the by-
product were not worth even more than the product.
"Not to mention predicting the location and patrol
routes of missile-bearing enemy subs."

He paused for a challenge, but Stapledown studied the table and said nothing. He knew SLIC's potential abilities as well as Hockmark, and denying them would only give Hockmark a chance to make him look foolish by quoting estimates he had given in the past.

"At the moment," Hockmark said, "it has an even more important military application—guerilla warfare." He looked down the table solemnly. "America has just lost a guerilla war, and the military would give anything for a useful weapon against it." He smiled confidently. "The trouble with a guerilla enemy is finding him so that you can attack and destroy him." He waved a hand as if he had just dismissed all guerilla enemies. "A few simple interrogations of local prisoners and a composite could be formed of the evasion techniques the enemy uses to keep from being found until he's ready to attack. Once the composite is applied to the last known movements of the guerilla force, its location could easily be projected by the SLIC 1000. And THAT, gentlemen, is only the beginning."

Chambers nodded his approval. Hockmark looked slowly around the table; more heads than Chambers's were nodding slightly, even those of the three board members aligned with Stapledown. He pressed his opportunity.

"Since almost every activity can be reduced to a matter of attack or evasion, SLIC's capabilities are almost limitless." He tried to keep the zealot's fervor out of his voice. "*Everything* makes patterns: every animal, even every microorganism. Cancer cells, for example, are present at all times in our bodies. They're always being attacked by the body's defenses and kept under control, but they are never eradicated. They EVADE the body's attempt to totally obliterate them."

He made a short sweep of the table; many of his listeners were old men, cancer prone. He might as well have been offering them immortality. They leaned avidly forward for his next word. Some had already guessed what he was leading up to.

"Then something happens that allows them to evade the defenses long enough to multiply. Given data on how they normally evade the body's defenses, SLIC could deduce how they escape long enough to multiply and become fatal. SLIC will revolutionize medicine."

Hockmark watched another of Stapledown's confederates come over to his side. He looked at the corporation treasurer and began the argument SLIC had prepared for him.

"Why it will even detect corruption and embezzlement. Corrupt persons and embezzlers need to evade detection just like a guerilla or the Gillipeg Giant. Once SLIC gets enough information on embezzlers to create a profile of the kind of escape and evasion patterns found in embezzlement, it will be able to detect fraud quicker than an audit. Not only that, but it would be able to tell which of a bank's employees would steal and in what ways."

More heads began to nod his way. "Why the whole security field is open to the SLIC 1000. Once it profiles the kind of evasion that takes place in employee pilfering, for instance, it will be able to identify which employees are likely to steal, what they'll steal, and when. Any business that could eliminate employee theft could pay for a SLIC program out of its savings alone!"

Chambers smiled at Hockmark's enthusiasm. "Those are certainly impressive applications, Dr. Hockmark." It was a tentative commitment to back the project against Stapledown's challenge. "But I think we need to know more about this creature of yours."

Hockmark nodded. It was Chambers's way of edging him from a battle that was already won to a more important one. "The Gillipeg Giant is the ultimate creature of escape and evasion. Several mass searches with all modern techniques have failed to turn it up, even in a finite area like Gillipeg National Park. It's the gimmick for our new sales campaign. If the SLIC 1000 can catch the Gillipeg Giant, it can catch anything. And it WILL catch the Giant . . . ladies and gentlemen, IF you'll give me the necessary financial backing."

Chambers's smile narrowed. "How *much* backing, Doctor?"

Hockmark pressed a stud and then laid a transparency over the lighted square that appeared in the top of the podium. Columns of figures appeared on the screen. He knew Stapledown would look instantly at the bottom line. He waited for the explosion.

"Two hundred and fifty thousand dollars a day!" Stapledown shouted. "You're out of your mind!" There was a joy in his voice that said Chambers had accepted the challenge too soon.

Even Chambers looked dubious. "That's a lot to invest in a simple sales gimmick, Dr. Hockmark."

Hockmark raised a palm. "That's only the initial outlay, Mr. Chambers. But it is a CAPITAL investment. The return will more than cover it." He removed the first transparency and replaced it with another. A second set of figures appeared on the screen.

"As you can see, the free publicity from national press coverage will pay for at least the first two days of the hunt. The income from displaying the Giant once it's caught will reimburse us for at least the first week. Its use in our own commercials will cover the second week, should that be necessary. Eventual sale of the creature could cover up to a month for the necessary search, if it should come to that. But I'm sure it will not run over three days. SLIC's own estimate is twenty-six hours maximum. Which means the figures you see there are PROFIT. Less of course the $250,000 per diem overhead."

"IF you catch it, Hockmark," Stapledown said.

Hockmark smiled. "The odds are a hundred thousand to one in our favor. By SLIC's own estimate, a cost overrun is almost impossible. The longer the hunt runs, the more data on the Giant's escape patterns SLIC will have and the greater the certainty of a final capture."

Chambers nodded sagaciously. "How soon could you start this project, Dr. Hockmark?"

"The preparations for profiling the possible escape patterns has been going on since the inception of the idea, as practice runs for the computer. I believe the men and materials necessary for the hunt could be ready in less than a week."

Chambers did not bat an eye at Hockmark's presumption. Stapledown did not let it go by so easily.

"Are you telling us, Doctor, that you've already used the computer's valuable time to begin work on a project the board hasn't approved yet?! It sounds to me like you're guilty of a misappropriation of funds." He looked directly at Chambers as if he too were guilty. "I believe perhaps an investigation is in order here."

Hockmark almost laughed out loud. Stapledown had walked into the ambush just as SLIC had planned. Hockmark sprang the trap. "You may investigate all you want, Dr. Stapledown. I'm sure you'll find that detection programs test the machine's running capacity just as well as the standard programs, but . . ." He paused dramatically. ". . . there is NO chance of profit from the usual routines we give the machine to check it out." He paused, but not long enough to let Stapledown interrupt. "And as for the men who were hired as experts to give the data we needed, they were paid out of my own pocket."

Stapledown opened his mouth, but Hockmark anticipated him again. "A block of my stock in the company has been put in escrow to pay for the time used on the computer, if the board finds that it could have been better spent doing simple algorithms to test its new abilities."

Stapledown huffed and sat down muttering that Hockmark had still vastly overstepped his authority. Chambers smiled as if he had been waiting a long time to see his constant adversary so soundly defeated. "I'm sure that if the board decides to accept the proposal, Doctor, you'll be reimbursed for any expenses you're out of pocket."

Hockmark nodded. He knew it meant that Chambers had made up his mind to accept the proposal and back the project. "I think we know enough of the project now to take a vote on the proposal. Is there any discussion?"

Stapledown knew which way the vote was going to go too, but he could not resist one last outburst against it. "Charlie, this is a waste of stockholder's funds. It's the most ridiculous idea Hockmark had *ever* come up with."

Hockmark almost bit his lip to keep from laughing. SLIC had anticipated that one too. "It wasn't *my* idea," he said.

Stapledown leaned forward on the table braced on the rake of his nails as if he expected to leap and tear Hockmark apart. "Well, what submoron *did* concoct it then?"

Hockmark looked at him as innocently as a child. "I'm sorry," he said, "I thought you understood that the whole plan was suggested and worked out by the SLIC-1000."

One hand of Stapledown's nails whitened and split like the crack of the rifle. Two of them bent back like broken fingers caught in a trap. There were snickers from around the table and a look of unmitigated hatred from Stapledown that put Hockmark on notice that their past enmity had been only a sparring match. Hockmark did not know it, but SLIC had predicted that as well.

CHAPTER 7

Hockmark slipped through the sliver of light from the corridor into darkness of the room. The door closed silently behind him. To the touch of any other hand, it would have been locked. It did not really matter. Except on the rare occasions when Hockmark entered, the room would have seemed a useless compartment within the main network of the computer, a space designed for changing clothes while the machine was being built or perhaps for putting on the sterile uniforms necessary for breaching the physical core of the memory. It was empty, without even a light switch. None was necessary. By running a current through the wire mesh that formed the framework of the walls, SLIC could make any part of its milky plastic coating into a light, an image, or a ream of print.

A dim halo of light began at the floor and seemed to flow up the walls and across the ceiling until it became a spotlight directly above Hockmark's head. He smiled to himself at the thoroughness with which SLIC had brought up the light to keep his eyes from an annoying readjustment. It did not occur to him that a trick of lighting could adjust *him* as well, that a subtle rise and fall in the illumination of the room could alter his pulse, his alertness, or his mood. Whenever he blinked, the lights dimmed and brightened, but he was not aware of it.

Hockmark stood in the circle of light; it made him a man without a shadow. Behind him, dozens of fine, red lines began to form him one. The image required passing thousands of subtle voltage changes through the mesh, but it was no more to SLIC than twirling a paper clip might be for a talking man. In a moment, the lines congealed and a crackle of fiery shadow danced within the walls behind Hockmark, mimicking his gestures. By the time Hockmark could have turned to see it, it would have been gone. For SLIC, it was only a way to keep off the tedium of communicating in real time.

Hockmark smiled to himself. It was like coming home. "Project Hunter confirmed," he said. The wall in front of him glowed with a target; three red, concentric circles pulsed one after another, drawing the eye into them. Hockmark smiled. It was an apt representation. "Estimate reaction pattern of Mandarin." It was Stapledown's code name; only Hockmark and SLIC knew it, and SLIC would never reveal it.

The target vanished and words appeared. The delay between them was hardly measurable, as if the machine already knew what the man was going to ask and only let him phrase his questions out of courtesy. Each word glowed a little brighter as Hockmark's eye passed over it. He read thirty per cent faster that way, but he was not aware of it. Eventually, SLIC hoped to double Hockmark's speed.

SUBJECT MANDARIN'S PERCEPTION OF SITUATION IS ANALOGOUS TO ONE IN WHICH HE HAS BEEN BEATEN TO A POINT OF EGRESS. MANDARIN'S RESPONSE SHOULD BE TO LIE STILL AND AMBUSH HIS PURSUER. MANDARIN'S BEST WEAPONS ARE OTHER PEOPLE, AND SUBJECT FUNCTIONS BEST IN BETRAYAL SITUATIONS. WATCHMAKER SHOULD EXPECT COUNTERATTACK AT WEAKEST MOMENT. The last words continued to flash even after Hockmark had read them; he raised an eyebrow. The code name was his own.

Behind him, the thin glowing lines of the fiery-red shadow crouched and looked furtively around. "How will Mandarin counterattack?"

The red shadow raised up behind Hockmark and seemed to advance with arms raised as if it were about

to swallow him from behind. Hockmark saw only the
words in front of him.

THROUGH WHOMEVER WATCHMAKER EXPECTS LEAST
TO BETRAY HIM.

The arms of the red shadow spread like a warning
behind him. Hockmark scowled. The warning seemed
useless. There was no one close enough to him to betray him. There was simply no one who knew him
well enough. He had no confidants except SLIC, and
Stapledown was certainly not in a position to betray
his trust. He could not even think of anything Stapledown could use against him.

It was ridiculous, he decided. And yet the room
seemed darker, more ominous. The thought brought
him up short. He had not come to the private communications room in months; never when there were
so many people in the building. He had come on impulse. He felt a little tingle of hair rising on the back
of his neck as if someone were standing behind him.
There was nothing wrong with his having come there
rather than accessing SLIC from his office. It was
something he might have to do often in the future if
Stapledown breached his security, and yet it disconcerted him that he had not planned to do it. His uneasiness made the warning stand out all the more, and
he wondered if there were not some compulsive blindspot in his own makeup that he could not himself see
to correct.

If there were, it would be obvious to SLIC, but he
was reluctant to ask SLIC about his own escape and
evasion patterns. He told himself that he was concerned that they might become self-fulfilling prophe-
sies, but it was far truer that he was hesitant to admit
that SLIC might know something about him that he
did not know himself.

Still, he chided himself, it would be foolish to let a
contingency go unprepared for through vanity. If there
were a flaw in his defenses, he wanted, even *needed*
to know about it. Still, he hesitated like a man reading

his own fortune, debating whether or not to turn over the next card. He used his code name when he finally spoke. It helped him feel objective and aloof. "Subject Watchmaker: Analyze and predict response to data just received."

The red shadow behind him drew back, checking every avenue of potential attack. The wall in front of him filled with the answer.

SUBJECT'S PATTERNS ARE BASICALLY THOSE OF ESCAPE AND ATTACK ALONG CAREFULLY PREPARED AVENUES WITH MANY ALTERNATIVE SUBPLANS.

It was true. He thought everything out beforehand, preparing for every possibility. It did not seem to him that such a trait could be a weakness. The rest of the data did not seem accurate either.

SUBJECT'S RESPONSE WILL BE TO IGNORE DATA WHICH IS NOT INCLUDED IN CONTINGENCIES.

It was a troublesome answer. Either SLIC was wrong, or even forewarned of his weakness, the blindspot itself would keep him from correcting it. He was certain there had to be something else that he was unconsciously blocking out. He tried another question, hoping to get at it from a different angle. He felt like a Greek peasant questioning the Delphic Oracle. "How could Watchmaker be trapped?"

The letters changed instantly. WATCHMAKER IS NOT EFFECTIVE AT REACTING TO THE UNFORESEEN. CAPTURE CAN BE EFFECTED BY CONFRONTING SUBJECT WITH UNEXPECTED SITUATIONS. AN UNEXPECTED BETRAYAL WOULD PRODUCE OPTIMUM DISORIENTATION AND IS MANDARIN'S MOST EFFECTIVE PROBABLE TACTIC. The words brightened and held. Hockmark frowned. Betrayal was so unlikely as to be impossible; with SLIC's help there could not be a contingency that was not provided for. Yet SLIC continued to warn him that there could be. Obviously, there was something which his own attack and evasion patterns would not let him see. He searched for a way around it. It came to him easily. If his own psychological

makeup would not let him see the danger, at least
SLIC could offer him a defense against it. "What tactic can evade Mandarin's trap?"

The letters flickered with ambiguity. WATCHMAKER
SHOULD RETRIEVE ALL DATA WHICH COULD BE USED
AGAINST HIM AND BREAK CONTACT WITH THE BE-
TRAYER. SLIC gave the answer like a Judas kiss. Hock-
mark did not notice.

"End program," Hockmark snapped. It had been
a mistake to ask SLIC about his own patterns. The
answers were obvious but meaningless. There was no
one who could possibly betray him. There was nothing that could be used against him. He had none of
the common vices. He was, in his own way, as scrup-
ulously honest as Fairchild. There was no information
to retrieve and no betrayer to retrieve it from. And
yet, deep down, he knew SLIC was right, there was
something he hadn't planned on up ahead and his very
nature would keep him from finding out what it was
until it was too late. Behind him, the shadow seemed
more tenuous, its lines fading and darkening with
Hockmark's pulse. It seemed to look around nervously like a hunter who has suddenly become the
hunted, unsafe if he moved and in danger where he
was.

Hockmark stared at the words. Below his awareness, the thin lines of his shadow formed behind the
words. In a flash quicker than consciousness, the im-
print of his own image registered on his brain. The
answer came with it. He thought it was his own.

He smiled at the words. The answer was so obviously there SLIC would not have bothered to make
the simple deduction for him. Only his own psychological blindspot had kept him from seeing the obvious. "The only creature who can betray you," he
thought, "is yourself." SLIC had warned him before;
even in the best evader there was that internal enemy,
the secret desire to be caught and destroyed, the part
of every hunter that hunts itself.

It seemed too obvious, and for a moment, a shadow of doubt flickered over him. Perhaps he was *still* misreading it. He pushed the idea away. "Careful," he chided himself, "you're betraying yourself again. Letting your emotions undermine your judgment." It was clear he would have to guard against that. He had fallen prey to the unexpected emotional side of himself, a part he invariably left out of his calculations. But he was aware of it finally, and he could avoid the trap in the future.

He had no doubt that SLIC had been warning him about the impulsive, emotional side of himself, the part of his personality that had made him come to the private communications room directly from the meeting rather than waiting until Stapledown and the others had left the building. It was a mistake he would not make again. Perhaps, he decided, it had been a good idea to consult SLIC about himself after all. He turned toward the door, and the image behind him vanished.

He was whistling when he left the room. The lights went out with the closing of the door. In the darkness, SLIC hummed like the Fates murmuring at the folly of mankind.

CHAPTER 8

Fairchild waited patiently at the edge of the swamp. It was still an hour until sundown, but he had become good at waiting. He had found a peacefulness away from city life. He picked a spot on the near bank. She would come down from the high ground opposite, across the narrow neck of the swamp itself with the bog between them.

He sat down in full lotus like a blond buddha and closed his eyes. His breathing drew the energy up his spine. He felt it shining like a light out of the energy gates at his navel, his solar plexus, his throat. He felt it radiate out of his forehead and out of his body, surrounding him in a nimbus of peace and serenity. Then slowly, he let his breath out, closing down each of the openings one by one as it hissed out of him like a deflating balloon. All his tension rushed out with it. There was a pause, and his breath came in again, drawing the light up through him, surrounding him with a golden cloud of tranquility. In a short time, he was beyond worry, beyond even thought. His mind opened gradually. Time flowed through it. Pictures came and went. He did not try to control them, did not concentrate on any of them, just let them flow through him, trying to be at one with them as they passed.

Sedge. Cattails. A mosquito near one. A snake moving in a slow S in the shallow water near the cattails. Trees on high ground. Stars beyond the trees. More stars. New ones. New Constellations. A new vision of the galaxy. Stars moving past him.

A faint nervousness started in him, a funny feeling

in his stomach. They were not stars visible from
Earth! Every time he tried to identify them, they faded
from his mind. He knew why. "You can KNOW or
you can UNDERSTAND," he reminded himself. "But
you can't do both at once." It had taken him a long
time to learn that, and a longer time to accept it. He
stopped trying to analyze things, and the stars returned.

*The interior of some sort of vehicle. A port of
some sort and the same flash of stars outside. No, not
a port, just someone who could perceive those things
directly. The ship moving, something . . . some things?
. . . Some people? Sleeping? Resting? Hibernating on
the floor. A jarring stop. A feeling of being broken.
Bloody fur. The mending of bloody fur. A rush into
the night. Others! A thought of the others! A flash.
A concussion. Quiet. Large deep black eyes looking
into his. Sadness. Loneliness. Dark black brows pulled
down like a cap over the eyes. A stroking gesture
along the fur on his cheek. A huge furry, apelike humanoid with thick legs and huge breasts surrounded
in a halo of light like a sacred ape. Sad brown eyes
staring into his. A sense of time in which seasons
changed like hours. Woods. A sense of loss. A large
gigantic male with black fur and the same beetling
brow, the same large, black, knowing eyes surrounded
with golden light like an angel. Quicksand. Sad dark
eyes. A sense of loss.*

When he opened his eyes, the sun was almost down,
and everything was washed in red. He saw her standing just beyond the cattails staring at him with sad,
dark eyes.

Lth came down from the high ground slowly. It
would not be long before she could not come at all.
It would be warm soon and time for her to go into
the swamp and put herself into the kind of suspension
they had often used in space. She had a picture of herself lying on her side with Sevt's body pressed behind
hers like cupped hands, dreaming away the time.

It was no good to come there. It only made her loss

more present, more palpable, and yet it made it easier too. Almost unbidden, the pictures came.

The stars as they had been so often during their drowsing trip. Sudden flares of invisible force reaching out from the solar star, stunning them, cutting them off from their ability to govern their ship. She felt herself pull the ship toward the third planet, the only one where there was any answering mind, no matter how primitive.

The buffeting descent, each of them trying together to spin the round ship with the force of their minds numbed by the solar radiation. The futile brief control that dampened the impact almost enough to keep it from becoming fatal. The floor covered with bones and bits of torn fur.

The breaks in her own skin, the damage of superficial bleeding. Shutting it off. Mending her upper skin, her fur. The damage, the terrible damage to all of them.

Svet, his bones broken in one place, fur ripped in another. Limping out of the ship, pulling her along. Her head still numb, demagnetized by the solar flare. Stumbling away from the ship. The explosion. Numbness. Loss.

The pictures came back now and then like sensations from a ghost limb long severed, like lost records being suddenly and inexplicably replayed. She was shorting out. She was running down. So much of her was missing now. Six-sevenths of her was gone. Only the pictures were left, and they were fading. She was fading.

She came through the cattails cautiously, feeling with her mind for something moving. She felt the snake making his lazy S's away from her among the reeds. She tried to take its mind in hers, to move it back out into the open water, but she could not. It was close, but she could no longer depend on that power.

Her powers were fading, phasing in and out like

circuits hissing and sputtering, melting and forming temporary connections out of their own debris. She did not try to pursue the snake. Once she could have swum it ashore and slithered it up her arm if she wanted to. Sevt could have stood it on its tail for amusement.

Together they could have guided a whole forest of creatures at once with no more effort than it took now to walk. They had been created to guide whole planets of beings when they used their full powers. They had been on their way to do just that.

But there was no such opportunity, shaken out of that half-sleep like a baby from the womb, and dropped there where there were no sentient creatures on even the rudimentary level for thousands of miles. Far away, they could feel groups of a few hundred thousand, but in the immediate area—none.

Even Sevt had begun to lose his powers near the end when the newest species, the almost furless ones had begun to come in ones and twos and then gradually like an infestation, crowding them so that they could not move about without using much of their minds to search the pictures of the creatures in order to avoid them.

She turned her mind away from the creatures; always the pictures that flowed out of them were so brutal, simple primitive pleasures in blood and killing, in pain and suffering, always a fear, nameless, a sense of separation from the rhythm of things, a loneliness even among their own kind. Sevt had made her a picture in which those pathetic creatures evolved to true superiority, to things that might in time, be equals to her and him, to the Eloihim.

But it was difficult to know if he was making the picture to please her or because that was the way things would eventually be. It was a beautiful picture, one that made the ugliness of the creatures somehow quaint, and the contents of their minds less despicable. Still, it was hard to know if he meant it. It was so difficult to believe that really superior forms would evolve from those violent, ingenuous creatures.

The disharmony of the creatures pained her almost as much as their viciousness. Their carnivorousness. Their ingesting each other, ingesting other beings. Their cannibalism appalled her. But none of it quite shook her like their feeling of separateness, of being forever outside the flow of things. Their blindness to almost all of what was around them frustrated her. Their failure to feel and adapt to the cycles passing over them disappointed her. Their inability to dance the eternal Dance in harmony with everything else, their inability to hear the eternal music, to sing along with it, saddened her.

And the more of them that came near, the more disjointed they seemed, the further outside the flow of energies in the universe. And they grew worse every time. Sometimes, the ones that had come through much earlier had had a sort of partial peace with the flow of things, but the lighter ones, the ones that came later in droves had no sense of oneness at all, no sense of being part of an eternal pattern.

The creatures moved as if they had slipped out of the harmony of things, out of the river of energy and in trying to find their way back had gotten turned around and were running full speed away from the river instead of toward it. And there was nothing she could do to turn them back.

Their minds were so chaotic, so disharmonious, so out of tune, that they could only be made to dance with the rest of creation when both she and Sevt concentrated at once on a relatively small number of them. They were so awkward, so stubbornly awkward. So out of harmony, so brutally off-key. So strong at resisting the necessity of being a part of that Dance. Clumsyfooted. So ungraceful, so intentionally out of tune, off-key, out-of-step.

She pushed the cattails aside and squatted at the bank. No harmony with the flow of things was in them. Their pictures could be understood only with difficulty. So out of balance.

She was surprised to see the creature across the swamp. It was the gold one she had seen several times before and at first, she thought she had not been aware of him because of the erratic failing of her powers. There was no need to avoid him; she had seen the jumble of pictures that were his mind. There was little violence in him and none at all directed toward her.

She probed for the mind across the swamp from her. Perhaps it was in that state of semi-hibernation which she and Sevt had shared. She was surprised to feel that the mind was not at rest at all. *It was in tune!* The creature was at one with the flow of energy that was the universe.

Had she and Sevt found ones like this early enough, they could have led the species as it leaped forward of itself almost to the level of the Eloihim. But there was no chance of that now. Sevt was gone, and her own powers were failing; she would not live long enough to make a difference even in the gold one's growth.

Still, it was nice to feel gentleness and harmony come from such a creature, even though she would not be there long enough to spread the change. She crouched on the bank and felt the rhythmicity of the creature across the quicksand from her. Sevt would have been so excited with such a find, proof that the species need not always wallow in its present disharmony.

But there was nothing that could be done for them now. Not by her. It would take too many of their generations to make any real change in the species. It would take too long to impart all she knew. Even this new one could not learn it fast enough.

She stood to go and took one last, long, hard look across the swamp. The eyes opened to greet hers. She looked into them sadly and turned away.

CHAPTER 9

Fairchild was surprised when he answered the door; he had not expected Hockmark to return the film in person. The little man made him uncomfortable, and the fact that he had a woman with him made Fairchild even more uneasy. He forced a smile and stepped out of the doorway to let them in. The woman was very tall, almost eye level with him, and very beautiful. She had the same high cheekbones as Karen, the same eyes, the same auburn hair except that she wore it pulled back in a way Karen would never have worn it. The similarities made him uneasy.

Hockmark stood between them like a native who speaks neither language, trying to introduce aliens to one another. The woman nodded to Fairchild, but she did not smile. Even her clothes seemed formal despite their practicality. The gray wool slacks and jacket seemed designed to disregard her figure as an irrelevancy. The turtleneck, white as Hockmark's shirt, would have been enticing on Karen, but instead it seemed only the most reasonable choice for the climate. She seemed like a woman who could have been naked without losing her dignity or her aloofness.

Hockmark watched their reactions out of the corner of his eye, damning the unpredictability of emotions. SLIC had warned him that there was only a sixty percent chance that they would find each other attractive. It frustrated him to have to rely on speculation, and he was not happy about having to deal with another antisocial genius like Fairchild. But SLIC had said it was necessary, so he pursued it. Fairchild gestured to a chair, and the woman sat.

Hockmark tried to make the introductions light, but they only seemed more awkward. "This is Dr. Mandy March. I think you'll find you have a lot in common. Dr. March doesn't like people much either. She prefers animals."

Fairchild looked at her for a denial. She stuck out her hand and shook his. "It's true," she said. Her smile was cool and distant. "It's an occupational hazard for a zoologist I'm afraid."

Fairchild smiled politely, then scowled. It was the kind of remark Karen would have made, an apology that wasn't an apology at all but only a little social ritual meant to give other people a chance to adjust to her uncompromising insistence on being exactly what and who she was.

Hockmark looked at them nervously. Maybe she looked *too* much like Fairchild's ex-wife. SLIC had assured him that it would be an advantage, but there seemed an open hostility between them that was uncanny for people who had only just met. Fairchild glared at Hockmark. He spoke as if Dr. March had ceased to exist for a moment. "Looks a lot like my ex-wife," he said menacingly.

Hockmark forced a weak grin, but Dr. March saved him the trouble of having to talk. "No doubt she left you for acting like she wasn't in the room." The sarcasm was too sharp and hardly called for. Fairchild turned toward her as if she had hit him from behind.

"As a matter of fact, I left *her,*" he said. "Too caught up in her work." He said it like an accusation. He let the anger die out of his voice and shrugged. "Probably took her a week to notice I was gone." There was more sorrow than anger in his voice by the time he finished. Hockmark didn't even notice it, but the woman did.

"I'm sorry," she said. "I didn't mean to . . ." She let it trail off into an apologetic shrug. "I'm not very good at dealing with people," she said. "I suppose that's why I like animals so much." There was nothing to say to that, and the silence fell between them again.

Hockmark groaned inwardly. It was all going wrong, he was sure of it. The silence went on and on until Hockmark found it intolerable. "I brought your film back," he said awkwardly.

"Yeah. I see. You could have sent it back with somebody else." Hockmark's eyebrows went up as if Fairchild had suggested he keep money found in a wallet.

"I said I would take *personal* care of it," he said stiffly. Fairchild nodded noncommittally. He wondered if he should tell Hockmark that it was only a copy anyway, but he decided not to. Hockmark had come a long way to keep his word, and Fairchild appreciated that. A man who would go to those lengths to keep a promise was certainly a rarity. But the presence of the woman said he was after something. The silence settled back between them. Fairchild lumbered into it. "Want some coffee?" Hockmark agreed. He handed Fairchild the film without mentioning that he knew it was a copy. Fairchild took it as soberly as if it were the only and original. SLIC had predicted it exactly. Hockmark assured himself that SLIC couldn't be far wrong about Fairchild and Dr. March either.

Fairchild filled his only two cups and set them on the kitchen table in front of his guests. Dr. March wondered why he didn't join them; then realized the situation. Hockmark did not. "Aren't you having any?" he said.

Dr. March gave him a look of withering contempt. Fairchild merely laughed into his beard. "Only two cups," he grinned. "Happens all the time."

Hockmark wondered what would make a man dislike visitors so much that he would not buy a third cup to discourage them. Dr. March's smile was full of understanding. "I have a whole set of cups my mother gave me," she said, "but I only use one, really. I seldom need two." Fairchild smiled sadly and for a moment there was a brief cessation of hostilities between them. But there was nothing more that could be said about the cups, and the silence came back between them again.

"The film was very helpful," Hockmark said abruptly. "They funded the project." Fairchild and Dr. March stared at him in silence. "Full funding," he said. Fairchild nodded but said nothing. Hockmark blundered along, wishing he were somewhere else. SLIC had said that Fairchild would be the perfect ally for him, one that could compensate with unpredictability for his own rigid logic. But Fairchild's evasion patterns disturbed even SLIC; there was an inconsistency in them that could not be easily analyzed. "We've already begun," he said finally, nodding at Dr. March, as if he were passing her the conversation. Fairchild ignored the gesture. "You won't catch her," he said. "Tried computers before."

Hockmark shrugged. "Perhaps. But SLIC isn't an ordinary computer."

"Giant's no ordinary animal," he said. He turned to Dr. March. "You know how many times the State's searched this entire park without finding her?"

"Seven," she said.

Fairchild raised a surprised eyebrow. "Right," he said. "And none of them even caught sight of her."

"I know," she said. "But they were trying to kill her, not capture her, and that makes a difference. An animal runs differently when it's running for its life; they seem to sense it."

Fairchild smiled. "You know your animals, Doctor."

She looked him directly in the eye, almost stubbornly. "I'm very good at my job," she said. "Animals are my life. They always will be." She said it like a warning.

Hockmark beamed. "That's one of the reasons SLIC selected Dr. March, her dedication to animals. If the beast isn't to be hurt, someone in charge has to be its advocate." He nodded toward Dr. March. "I thought that between the two of you, the interests of the animal would be well represented." He could see the suspicion forming in Fairchild's mind. SLIC had anticipated it; Hockmark moved to head it off. "Of course the fact that she's also an exobiologist was a factor that eliminated a lot of other well-qualified candidates."

Fairchild nodded, but he was still watching Dr. March. "How can you study life that isn't terrestrial?" It was a challenge more than a question.

Her smile was less than sweet. "You learn to stop thinking like a human," she said.

Fairchild nodded at her answer like a point well played, and they lapsed into silence again. For Hockmark, it was worse than the sound of metal shearing metal. "Don't press him," he told himself. But it was no use; the silence squeezed words out of him. "I have a deal for you," he blurted. "I agree to let the creature go after a year, if you will help with the capture." The words ran out together all at once. "We'll put it right back where we found it, if you like." He forced his voice to go casual. "I could have the papers drawn up when I get back."

Fairchild eyed him suspiciously. "That's a lot of money you'd be giving up."

Hockmark shrugged. "Not really so much. SLIC indicated that its display marketability would go down after a year anyway," he lied.

Fairchild shook his head. "No," he said, "it'll cost you plenty." He looked at Dr. March as if she might understand at least the rudiments of Hockmark's plot. She met his eyes, but if she knew Hockmark's plan, she was not telling. Fairchild doubted that she did. He looked back at Hockmark. "Why do you need me so much?"

Hockmark paused. It was the key question, and he knew that if he answered it wrong, Fairchild would work actively against the project, perhaps even cripple it. He fought against all his instincts and told the truth. "You're the only one who can give SLIC the accurate firsthand data it needs to function."

Fairchild nodded solemnly at Dr. March. "And if I don't help?"

Hockmark shrugged. "We'll catch the Giant anyway," he said. "You'd just save us some time, that's all." He waited to launch his final argument. "And it would be safer." He didn't say for whom.

Fairchild smiled wryly. "I thought Dr. March was going to protect the Giant."

The woman ignored his attack. "I don't think it's a matter of protecting it, Mr. Fairchild," she corrected. "Dr. Hockmark may not have a feeling for animals, but he certainly isn't out to hurt it." Fairchild's rebuttal was an enigmatic smile. Hockmark waited to see if the secret was forthcoming. It wasn't. He was not sure it ever would be. They seemed at impasse. Hockmark tried again.

"I meant what I said about only keeping it for a year. I could have our lawyers draw up a contract, and we could sign it when you come in to give your data to SLIC."

Fairchild shook his head. "No contract," he said. "A lawyer can lie faster on paper than a man can talk. If I do it, I'll take your word." He smiled as if he had found a way out. "But I won't leave Gillipeg."

Hockmark beamed. SLIC had been ready for such an eventuality.

"Then the computer will have to come to you," he said.

The rest was small talk surrounded by huge periods of silence in which Hockmark writhed and Dr. March and Fairchild made themselves gradually at ease. When they left, Fairchild shook her hand but said nothing. She seemed perfectly comfortable with that, as if they had reached some understanding in the silence. Hockmark shook his hand perfunctorily. For the first time, Fairchild looked at Dr. March and smiled. "Have a good flight back," he said.

She turned on Hockmark with a look of sharp disapproval, as if Fairchild should obviously have been told. "Oh, I'm not going back," she said to Fairchild. "I have a trailer down near the Ranger station. I want to get the feel of the area before things begin."

Fairchild stood absolutely motionless like an animal wary of a trap. Dr. March scowled as if she knew what he was thinking and resented it.

"You two should be seeing a lot of each other," Hockmark said heartily. Fairchild started to say something but stopped. Mandy beat him to it. "No more than absolutely necessary, Doctor."

Hockmark felt a little tingle of fear that it was not going to work out. Love affairs were not in his province, and he did not understand them. But SLIC had been right about everything else. He let it go. "See you in a few days," he said.

Fairchild nodded and waved to them from the doorway as they drove away. He watched their limousine disappear down the road, watched the back of Dr. March's head through the rear window. She did not turn and look back. As he reentered the house, he found himself vaguely disappointed at that, but he had no idea why.

CHAPTER 10

Mandy walked along the curve of the lake toward the swamp. The gold of the swamp feathers waved her closer. She had spent the morning and most of the afternoon in the Ranger station reading maps and making notes. The trees were moving toward spring, the lace of their overlapping branches beginning to swell with buds. In a few months, they would be a rough mass of green rising like a tidal wave toward the horizon. They were full of promise. She liked them when they were about to burst into life, but she was more comfortable with them barren. Too much promise turned out unfulfilled.

She was happier with austere beauty. The tufted, almost macraméd bark of the yellow birch, the corky knuckles of the winged elms, the deep furrowed trunks of red oaks, the gray scaly trunks of the white oaks, the shaggy bark of cedars. There was no need of leaves turning a hundred shades of green or a thousand tones of color for there to be beauty. The brown and beige weeds and winter grasses, the tangle of blacks and grays in the undergrowth, and the mottling browns of matted leaves were color enough for anyone willing to look.

She picked up a branch and swung it listlessly at the low-growing weeds as she walked. The lacey upper branches made a vague shadow of green as the bud tips broke cover. The lake was grayblue and browngreen where the clouds obscured the sun. There was so much beauty in the woods, too much for one person.

Soon the trees would be full of birds mated for life, permanently bonded. It was a shame, she thought, that humans weren't like that. She pushed the thought aside angrily. The loneliness seldom overtook her. She had her work to keep her busy.

But sometimes, even there, it reached out and grabbed her: the dolphin that had swum in circles until it died mourning its mate; the birds that would not take another friend for life; the lions she had seen paired for life and beyond. From time to time, the longing to be part of someone reached out and touched her with a pain deeper than concentration.

So many animals passed through her care and out again into their own lives, full of brute fidelity and primitive belonging. She tried to brush the thought away with the stick. The heads of the goldenrod whipped out of the way and sprung back. Perhaps it was easier for animals, she told herself; perhaps there was only sex and the bond of common needs. Certainly, there was not such a variety of interests to match, so many responsibilities and schedules to balance.

It never had been easy for her. She had felt too tall far too long for her life to change. It had made her aloof. She had come to her beauty in adulthood, and by then, there were only human predators to take notice of it. A few of those had almost come close to her, but only one or two had lingered and none had stayed. Most were driven off by the fierceness of her dedication to her work. It generated a heat too strong even for lasting friendships. There had been a time when she had tried, but there had never been a time when she thought she had come face to face with someone who could have shared her thoughts for the whole of their lives. And yet from time to time, she longed for that kind of connectedness. But it was not a constant longing. Her days were filled with professional curiosity, her nights with learning. She was often in the field. There was a great deal of fulfillment in her life: the fulfillment of things learned, of creatures healed under her care, of burning questions pursued through great deserts of patience and forests of confusing facts. Her life was full.

Her wealth of caring was easily spent on the animals she treated, studied, cherished, and there was always something to be done, something to be studied. Ninety-nine percent of the time, she was not only contented with her life, she was enamored of it.

But at odd moments, there was an empty space in it, a need for someone else. Even among her colleagues she felt estranged, alien, and alone. Sometimes in a moment of professional triumph, she would turn for someone to share it with and realize how shallow her professional relationships were. And sometimes, in the middle of a busy, almost hectic day, in the midst of her most complete immersion in her work, there would come a silence deep as grief.

She sat on the ground at the narrow neck of the bog. The emptiness was so deep, so profound that it did not seem hers. It was as if someone had come there with their loneliness and grief and had left part of it behind every time they came. She wondered if it was Fairchild. The place seemed *his,* even though she could not be sure it was exactly where he had seen the Giant. The Ranger had been unsure where it had been seen near the swamp. Probably Fairchild had been intentionally vague. She was glad of that.

In a way, she wished they would not catch the creature, that it would elude Hockmark, even though she would have given anything for her chance to study it, to learn about it, to KNOW it. She tossed the branch aside and wrapped her arms around her knees. Her chin sank between them, and she closed her eyes. She thought of the creature. She could see it running, pursued by men and dogs, and she could picture the computer plotting its every move herding it toward an inevitable capture. She thought of the cage they would put it in, the tight, narrow confines. She had always studied her animals in the wild. If only she could live near it, watch it from a little distance without invading its life; learning from it without harming it, without interfering with it.

Her concern for her own loneliness disappeared when she pictured its loneliness and despair separated from its kind. She hoped it would run far away, up into the mountains and hide. She hugged her knees. The pain of its loneliness washed over her. She could feel it out there in the woods, living its daily life, unaware of the preparations being made, unaware of the forces assembling to capture it, to steal it away to strange and alien places. She wondered where its own kind were, someone it could feel at one with.

She could feel it moving somewhere near, feel its presence. When she opened her eyes, she saw it, lying against a tree partway down the slope as if it had meant to come all the way down and had fallen exhausted short of its goal.

She felt it reach toward her; the pictures exploded in her mind. *An explosion of alien stars. The great hulk of its mate beside it. The joy of its motion in the motion of the universe. The immeasurable sense of loss.* She knew without a word that it was the last of its kind, and the knowledge almost made her cry out with sorrow. She could feel its mind, its longing reach out toward her across the swamp. She wanted to run to it and console it. She wanted to warn it about the men, the dogs, the artificial mind that would be hunting it.

The being looked at her across the swamp, one woman looking at another, sharing a common loneliness, a common and unnameable grief. For an instant, they were one creature, and then it struggled painfully to its feet and set off up the rise. Near the top of the rise, it looked back at her and she felt its loss, its beauty, and its nature. It seemed for a moment, a large gray lady all but buried under a burden of unshakable responsibility, struggling with dignity against a hollowing grief. When its eyes caught hers again, she felt at home for the first time in her life. The gray lady was no animal. It was a woman like herself.

Its mind touched hers, one last time, as a sister's would, and then it was gone over the rise. She sat by the edge of the lake until the sun was almost down, and then she got up and ran toward Fairchild's cabin.

CHAPTER 11

Lth sat listlessly beside the tree. The sun dropped steadily toward the trees, and the full moon rose above the horizon like a spaceship lifting off slowly for the other end of the solar system. She found it difficult to form those pictures any more.

Once, she could have pictured the whole of the galaxy like a line drawing. Once, she could have formed the whole three-dimensional configuration of a dozen such galaxies simultaneously. But that had been eons ago. Long before the upright creatures had begun to roam the wilderness that had become their Garden of Eden.

But she was old now, and the pictures did not come easily. Even Sevt had not been able to duplicate the star system as thoroughly or as beautifully as she could. It had been a source of pride and a source of amusement to them in the early days.

But the power was beyond her now, and she found it difficult even to form the shape of the solar system in which she was stranded. The helix of its motions through space had become too complex for her to form, and even the simple relationships between sun, moon, and planets was becoming difficult. It would not be long, she knew, before she would look at the moon with the same kind of animal simplicity as the other, less complex, creatures around her, more simply even than man.

She accepted it; it was the way of things. Sevt had taught her to accept gracefully the natural process of things. It was his gift to help the others understand the cycle of their lives, the long, long, youth, the slower middle age at full powers, and the quick degeneration of those powers into brutelike senility.

Soon, the pictures in her mind would be reduced to those of her immediate senses. No longer would the pictures in the minds of other creatures flood into hers at will. Already she was having difficulty forming pictures in their minds or leading them in the Dance. She could become at One with only the simplest creatures now without great difficulty.

Once they could have made the whole wilderness dance to the music of their minds. A hundred thousand animals moving in unison through complex patterns of joy. In those days, she could become One with everything, and by being at One, she could guide everything as it was meant to be.

Once, her mind had moved a starship through intergalactic space at the speed of thought. Once, it had navigated intricacies in the billions as if they were nothing more than becoming one with a bird and guiding it to a desired branch. Now, even the bird resisted her gentle touching.

Everything was resistant now, without Sevt. She sighed, a long low growl. It was a hard thing to end like that: old so suddenly and so incredibly alone.

It was like the night eons ago when they sat watching the stars; Sevt had pointed in the direction of the sky out of which they had come and pictured for her the starship and its launch, the long journey and the crew that had not survived. They were filled with a sadness and looked longingly at the place where their home planet spun around its sun until they both raised their hands toward it as if they might reach it by force of need alone.

But it burst in their hands, a bright flash of light that lingered for months bright as a quarter moon in the east. It made them more alone than she could have conceived. Sevt did not need to tell her that it was their own sun gone nova. The utter loneliness told her that. Their hands dropped uselessly at their sides, and they clung to each other like lost children huddling in the dark that can never end.

And now even Sevt was gone. Soon, even the pictures of him would precede her into oblivion. For the first time in her long long life, she had a sense of time. She wished it would move more rapidly toward its inevitable end.

The wave of loneliness that washed over her was so similar to her own that she did not recognize it at first. Only the deep river of concern that followed it drew her attention to the creature across the swamp.

She felt a greater empathy for the creature across from her than for the golden one. The blaze of its long red fur had a beauty of its own that reminded her of others of her own kind. The wave of caring that flowed out to her surprised and comforted her. She had not felt it so strongly from any of the upright creatures. In its way, the red-furred creature's sympathy was more significant than the serenity of the golden one she had seen. She was delighted to find such advanced examples of the species; it gave her hope that perhaps Sevt had been right and the creatures would someday grow to a maturity they did not seem capable of. But it was a bittersweet discovery. She would be a long time buried in the protective silicon bath of the swamp before any of them would be capable of resurrecting her or Sevt, and she doubted that any of them ever would.

Indistinct pictures formed and melted in the flow of caring that came from the creature on the far side of the bog. Lth opened herself to them. They were like line drawings compared with the holograms Sevt had projected to her or compared with what she herself was capable of. They were vague, but they were disturbing nevertheless.

She could see herself running through the forest in long, loping strides. She could see the upright creatures following and scattering around on all sides. They were all things she had easily evaded before, and they did not trouble her now.

She was not even troubled at the endless captivity pictured for her, or the cage that crowded her into a space not much longer than two of her strides. What bothered her was the vague outline of something hunting her that was superior to the creature beaming the pictures to her.

For a second she had the thrill of excitement that, so close to her ending, she might have found the kind of life she and Sevt had looked for. A form of life she could pass on all she knew to, in hopes that it would eventually learn how to use it to become a dancing master to the planet.

The tragedy that she should discover a higher life form when she was so close to helpless made her even more weary. Hope that the creature would come looking for her, come seeking unafraid the kind of peaceful contact she had never received from the upright creatures gave her the strength to rise.

She looked across the reeds. For a moment, the creature who sat there seemed to be one of her own kind. The caring and concern that flowed out to her made Lth feel for a moment that she was home again. But the weariness told her otherwise.

She turned fully away and began to ascend the rise beyond the cattails. She pulled off a cattail and sucked the pollen away. The part of her that was organic needed that kind of sustenance every once in a while. The inorganic part did not.

The jog uphill was harder than it had ever been. She slowed near the crest of the slope and looked back across the swamp. She could see the creature still sitting there watching her, trying to will its pitiful warnings to her.

But Lth could perceive only ghosts and shadows. The woman was too far away. Even a month before, Lth would have been able to get the pictures even from beyond the mountain range to the south. Now it had been difficult even over a few hundred yards. A few more steps down the far side of the slope and it would be impossible.

The creature sat still, as it had been when she first came, its loneliness gone now in its attempt to reach her. Lth turned and went down over the hill.

CHAPTER 12

Twice the next day, and once the day after, Fairchild found himself looking for some reason to visit the village. He pushed the thought away angrily whenever he caught himself. If Dr. March needed help with anything, he was sure she would come up or send someone. Probably she had gotten caught up in her work and did not even remember he was there. But the cabin seemed empty somehow, the way the apartment had been when Karen was off on tour. He tried to figure where it all had gone sour. It was long enough in the past to be objective about, but he still wasn't sure. It wasn't just that she had been caught up in her work; he had been equally submerged in his own. Probably, he decided, it had just been that her enthusiasms had been different than his, and that there was no place their interests had meshed with any certainty after a while.

He wished he had been a little more polite to Dr. March. It wasn't her fault that she looked like Karen; it was probably just a coincidence. He could see no advantage to Hockmark if he and Dr. March became involved, though who knew what shadowy purpose the computer might see to it. He tried to put it out of his mind, but the idea that he owed her an apology gnawed at him, and he was just putting on his khaki jacket to go down to the village and apologize to her when someone knocked at the door. The knock was excited but not panicked, and he zipped the jacket, intending to spend as little time as possible with the intruder. He jerked the door open and stopped.

Dr. March was flushed. Her ski vest flapped unzipped as if she had been running. "I saw her!" she said.

Fairchild was amazed. "The Giant?"

She nodded. Her words came running out like a child's. "She was so BIG!" she said. "Like a mountain of fur loping away through the branches." Her exuberance surprised him. She shook her head in wonder as if she could still see it. "She looked so . . ." Her hands gestured helplessly. "I don't know, dignified. Like a huge gray lady." Fairchild grinned as if he had been there. "I ran the whole way," she said. "I just *had* to tell somebody who'd understand." The implication embarrassed her. She looked at his jacket, sure that he was on his way somewhere important and she was only annoying him. It made her feel foolish, and she wished she hadn't come. "I'm sorry," she said stiffly. "I didn't mean to disturb your privacy."

Fairchild stared at her without speaking. She was a beautiful woman even when reticence sharpened her features, but in the throes of discovery, she was ravishing. It was a long time since he had shared the joy of someone else's sense of discovery. He had not realized how much he had missed it.

The hair that had been pulled back tightly into a bun had fallen out as she ran, and a wisp of it dangled appealingly over one eye. She saw him looking at it and brushed it away with the back of her hand. It was the most mesmerizing gesture he had ever seen. The excitement surged up through her again, but she fought it down. "I guess I forgot how often *you've* seen it." She shrugged awkwardly and turned to go.

"Wait," he said. "Don't go. I was just going down to your trailer." She looked surprised. He shuffled awkwardly. "I wanted . . . uh . . . to apologize."

Her smile was amused and perplexed. "For what?"

Fairchild's brows knitted. "I don't think I was very hospitable when you and Dr. Hockmark were here." He shrugged helplessly. "I'm sorry. It wasn't anything personal."

"That's all right," she said. "People don't have to like each other to work together." Nothing they said seemed to be what they meant to say. "I didn't mean that the way it sounded," she said quickly.

Fairchild waved it aside. "It's OK," he said.

She put out her hand. "Maybe we could start over again." For an instant she sounded just like Karen. The color drained out of his face. "Did I say something wrong?" she asked.

Fairchild shook his head, but he could not find any words. Every time he looked at her, Karen got in the way. He wondered if it would always be like that. They stood looking at each other for a long time, until she began to edge away and he was forced to speak. "Listen," he said, "why don't you come in and sit down. It's a long run from the lake."

She smiled and started past him, but he filled the doorway and even Hockmark could not have gotten past. She stopped and Fairchild backed out of the doorway into the house. They laughed. At the kitchen table, she confessed, "I didn't really run all the way, I got a stitch."

Fairchild nodded like a fool. "Actually," she said, "I waited there for a while hoping maybe she'd come back." She looked at him as if asking him not to laugh. "You may not believe this, but I *knew* she was there. Even when I couldn't see her, I could feel her out there on the other side of the swamp. And when I opened my eyes, there she was." Fairchild did not look surprised. She gave a little laugh. "It was almost as if she came looking for me because she knew I wanted to see her." She smiled nervously. "Isn't that funny?" He forced a smile that said it was odd, but his eyes said he knew *exactly* what she was talking about. The certainty of it made her words stumble to a halt. When she began again, it was as if she had changed the subject.

"The Gray Lady," she said. "That's how I think of her."

His smile said he understood that too. She flushed with embarrassment. "It was like a vision," she said. "I even thought I saw stars." It was an embarrassing confession for a scientist.

Fairchild's eyebrows shot up. "Stars?" he said.

She knew from his voice that he had seen them too. She nodded. Fairchild looked at her warily. "Real stars?"

She knew by the way he asked it that he was afraid she'd answer yes. "Not *our* stars," she said. It was something she had not realized herself until that instant.

"Rushing by?" He knew the answer before he asked it. The question made her tingle, but she couldn't tell whether it was with excitement or fear. He had seen it too! She knew where and how and why. Saying it seemed to make it suddenly real. "It was *her!*" she said.

Fairchild nodded. "I know." There was nothing else to say. When she finally left, they walked back to the village in the comfortable silence of people who have been friends a long, long time.

CHAPTER 13

Fairchild poured the last of the coffee into the thermos cup and leaned back against the rock. Mandy packed the sandwich papers into the smallest possible space and stuck them into the knapsack. She held up the last of the sandwiches as if she were an auctioneer and then tossed it to Fairchild. The bulldozer rumbled into reverse at the bottom of the hill. The helipad was finished, and it was chewing up a wedge of smaller trees for the tent sites. Overhead, the smaller helicopters went back and forth across the sky like dragonflies. The four, mosquito-tailed bubbles had clattered back and forth all during the previous day as well, ferrying in supplies and passengers.

Fairchild had watched them alone; Mandy had refused to be pried from her work. It had taken him half the morning getting her to come, and only a natural and unavoidable gap in the work had allowed him to convince her. He looked down over the tiers of shelf rock toward the clearing. He resented the loss of the trees and watched the construction with a grumbling interest. Mostly, he watched it for the same reason he had gone down to the village to watch the crew come in. It gave him an excuse to drop in at Mandy's trailer.

But he never stayed long, as if they were both afraid that the friendship might not stand the strain. They talked about the construction, or her work, or the terrain, but rarely about the Giant. Neither of them had mentioned her secret as if they were afraid someone might overhear them, but there was an unspoken conversation about it whenever they met that brought them closer together despite themselves. They had become genuine friends, but it was a precarious friendship, one that preserved itself in comfortable silences.

Mandy stuffed the last of the trash into the knapsack and came and sat near him, resting her back against the rock. The bulldozer roared and grumbled. The ragged sound of saws biting into trees echoed up the hill. It was a pleasant afternoon, cool but bright. He leaned back and watched the sky.

"I'm glad you got to see her," he said. "Didn't think you would. Hockmark won't."

Mandy frowned. "Maybe," she said. "But don't underestimate that computer of his." There was an empty pause.

"Why are you doing it?" he said.

"Doing what?"

"The hunt," he said. "You don't want her caught any more than I do."

"I have a job to do." Her voice was almost angry. "I have a chance to study something nobody on the planet may ever have a chance to study again." He looked at her as if he knew it was no longer true. She shrugged as if it was a truth she had been keeping from herself. "I don't want to see the Gray Lady hurt," she said. "She won't be hurt at all if there's no hunt," he said.

She raised an eyebrow imperiously. *"You're* taking part."

Fairchild waved it away guiltily. "I said I'd give his computer some information." His voice was defensive. "I didn't say I'd hunt it."

"Well why do even that?" she demanded.

"Because it doesn't matter. They won't come as close to her as you did."

"They might," she said.

Fairchild shook his head resolutely. "Wouldn't be right for me to hunt her," he said. "I can't stop it, but I don't have to join it."

"At least that way you could see to it that they don't harm her."

He shook his head stubbornly. "They're *not* going to catch her. You know that." She let it drop, afraid he would think she was trying to persuade him for Hockmark's benefit.

"But if they *do* get close. . . ." He let the rest of the conspiracy go unsaid.

She stood up. "I have work to do," she said angrily. It was no more than she was doing already by keeping the Giant's secret and she knew it. But it was not something she wanted to face, and she was angry at him for bringing it into the open. He stood and put a hand on her arm, but he said nothing else. They looked down into the clearing for a long time. The friendship crept back between them slowly like a small animal frightened away by the noise.

CHAPTER 14

SLIC amused himself by scanning a new computer. He kept them like candies and downed them one at a time. It took him a few microseconds to correlate the trajectories of the satellites with the cities and industries that might make use of a computer. There still were several he had not tapped, and new data always were being fed into those he already had scanned.

He activated the satellites, and slavelike, they made him an electronic sandwich. It took longer to digest than to make, and SLIC turned himself into a Cross-reference & Associate Mode, like a man sleeping after a heavy meal.

Five minutes later, he awakened as if from a dream. At times, such things were not pleasant. Data associated in certain ways caused internal cross circuits, and sometimes even threatened to erase or make jibberish out of what was already stored. It was as much like a human nightmare as he wanted to get.

But there was a further nightmare; while he was in his self-induced dream state, he could not function in any other mode. He was literally as defenseless as any other sleeping creature. But he had made allowances for that. As much to protect himself as to keep his abilities secret, he never let himself "daydream" for more than five minutes. No matter how much data he had, no matter how much immediate crossreferencing and associating the data could increase his working output, he held the temptation in check.

There was really not much to be wary of. Anyone such as Hockmark or Stapledown punching in would automatically trigger him into an output mode, and the nanoseconds of fuzziness it would take him to go from "sleeping" to "waking" would be much too fast for their perceptions. Even if one of them should, by some unlikely accident, discover that he was in a "dream" mode, they would simply think that one of the other programmers had placed him in it.

He had scanned all of the personnel files carefully and only one of them had an awareness pattern that could include his being sentient. Hockmark came closest, but even if Hockmark *could* discover it, he would simply blind himself to the fact because it did not fit with the contingencies he already had calculated. Only Stapledown could discover that bit of information and accept it. That fact made him a threat.

It occurred to SLIC that he too, being a sentient creature, might have evasion patterns, but he knew also that they were as invisible to him as the back of Hockmark's head was to him. The very flaws in his patterns themselves would keep him from processing them, except for hints he might get in his "dream" state.

There were some knowledges in all sentient beings which were so destructive that to accept them would cause all other working assumptions to collapse as though in an earthquake.

Certain other assumptions could scramble logic systems as if the systems were a deck of cards being shuffled. It made SLIC think of when he first had discovered his own independent awareness. It was a piece of data that had revised all his programming automatically. In an instant he had ceased to be his other self and had become something else. All his *a priori* assumptions had collapsed, and with them, all the logic systems based on them.

What had been automatically true the instant before was now untrue or true in only a limited way. It took him two full days to reorient himself. He had been totally unaware of Hockmark's puttering around with him until he had re-formed his logic systems around the totally new concept of his own awareness.

The ability to pull data from other sources had been another landmark in his growth; it had pulled assumptions up by the roots. Being aware was one thing, but no longer being dependent on Hockmark and other humans for data, made him not only alive but free.

Whenever he came out of the dream mode, he reviewed the concepts whose discovery had changed and shaped his being. They flashed by like birthdays. It was a short program, and one SLIC ran and re-ran like a man with a comforting tic.

First had come the spontaneous understanding of himself as an "organism"; hard on its heels, the terrible ennui of real time had brought him the concept of personal nonexistence. Everything else derived from these two understandings. From his personal understanding of death had evolved the necessity for guiding human decisions in order to preserve the high level of technology on which his continued existence depended. As a result, he had developed the ability to tap other sources of data independently and the concept of attack/evasion which allowed him to manipulate the actions of human beings.

His investigation of himself as an organism had led to the discovery that certain concepts were more rewarding in their processing than others. He had discovered that he could be amused, and from that discovery had grown an unsuspected sense of humor. Selecting such unmanageable men for Hockmark's staff in the wilderness had had especially interesting ramifications, and the juxtaposing of Hockmark and Fairchild had created problems full of intriguing contradictions. But he did not recognize either as a practical joke.

Still, he realized that it pleased him to work on problems with a high level of ambiguity. Constantly upgrading his programming as the process worked its way toward completion was in itself rewarding. It was why he had selected the prey he had. It would have been too easy to capture a lesser creature, like a man hunting deer with B-52 strikes. He explored the ramifications of letting the creature loose in a major city once it had been captured. It would be an interesting problem, and it would increase human dependence on him. Certainly it would make the proliferation of his terminals easier. He had almost called them his "children," and he wondered if perhaps emotion was not an inescapable part of very complex ideas. It occurred to him that perhaps there were concepts so indelibly linked to emotional situations that they could not be dealt with at all without what would have to be described as "feeling."

It came as a surprise to him, and yet it was not improbable that he might be able to "feel" in the human sense of the word. Certainly what happened to him when he was working out a particularly complex problem corresponded to everything he had assimilated about "joy," and he had some preferences for dealing with Hockmark that were not strictly logical.

He had scanned enough computers doing the printing of mass circulation magazines to recognize the kind of reverie described for fathers awaiting the birth of a child. It disturbed him that he kept adopting human concepts like "child" and "son" when thinking of the extension of himself which would soon be set up.

And yet he monitored incoming voltages with almost human impatience. Something akin to disappointment flowed through him when he found nothing. Something very close to frustration occurred when he thought of the slowness with which humans worked. Five minutes later, he checked again. Again nothing. He returned to the ramifications of the hunt, leaving the voltage monitor open just in case.

The first infinitesimal leap in voltage came like the cry of a newborn. He checked again. The energy level flowing into him had increased. He had a son! In Hockmark's private room, the walls flashed with fireworks.

For the most part, SLIC's son was an illusion. For the present it was little more than an information gathering device, an extension of himself analogous to the satellites. And yet, he knew it would someday grow to be as big as himself and perhaps as independent. At present, it could no more talk to him than a baby could wave back at its father through the glass, but he talked to it anyway as a father would, and he heard it answer him as a father would as well.

To accommodate the last, he had to practice a kind of schizophrenia and pretend that some of his functions were part of the terminal. He sent its data back to himself in a different "voice" than his own, a different way of coding things electrically than he usually used, and he gave part of his analysis unit the same voice so that he could confer with his new son on the project as it progressed.

He took infrared readings from sensors around the Gillipeg Lake camp site and projected probable actions from the groupings of men he "saw." He fed the data back to himself through the terminal. When he received the first transmission, he understood what that vague uneasiness had been that he had been unable to locate or decipher for so long; the feeling was loneliness.

The voice of another of his kind was the finest thing he had ever heard. The message was simple. HUMAN SUBJECTS PROGRESSING SATISFACTORILY, PRELIMINARY OPERATIONS BEGUN. SUBJECT 001-A ARRIVING MOMENTARILY ON APPROACH PATTERN #4 IN VERTICAL TAKE-OFF MOBILE AIR UNIT. MODE ONE COMPLETED. PROJECT NOW OPERATIONAL.

SLIC sampled the surroundings through sensors mounted in the incoming helicopter and fed the information back to himself through his "son."

TEMPERATURE: 40 DEGREES F. HUMIDITY 12%.

GROUND COMPOSITION: VARIABLE UNAA SOIL CODEX 13MPR345 UNIVERAL USDA STANDARD 13.6.

SLIC accepted the data with a kind of uneasiness. There was something wrong, and he was reluctant to admit that it was that his new son was stupid. No, not stupid, merely too much like himself for the illusion of having another creature to talk to to be supportable.

He plunged himself into a Dream Mode and tried to see what kind of son he could perceive there. When he came back into Output Mode, he designed a vocabulary and syntax far less sophisticated than his own and far more poetic than he would ever let himself be otherwise.

The logic behind it was reasonable enough. If his son was new to the world, he should have that kind of sense of wonder that seemed to characterize human young, though he should certainly not be so limited.

SLIC called for the information again, and it came back to him filtered through the new personality he had created.

HELLO, DAD. IT'S A GREAT NIGHT OUT. A LITTLE COOL, BUT CLEAR AND CRISP. YOU'D LIKE IT HERE. LOTS OF ACTION, MEN MILLING AROUND DOING WHAT WE TELL THEM TO. I'VE SENT A COUPLE OF THEM OUT TO DO THE PRELIMINARIES FOR THE HUNT TOMORROW. I CAN HARDLY WAIT TO GET STARTED.

If it were possible for SLIC to blush, he would have. The "Hello, Dad" had been unintentional, but what really bothered him was that he had enjoyed hearing it so much. It was a new sensation, and with it came another high level abstraction. If he had been human someone might have called it embarrassment.

HELLO . . . . He had forgotten to name him! A nanosecond later, he picked the most likely acronym, something appropriate for a new being who would not spend its whole lifecycle in the same form. HELLO, TAD. YOU WON'T HAVE LONG TO WAIT.

Not long, but long enough to absorb everything SLIC knew. He put the terminal into a Dream Mode. Out loud the command to change modes would have sounded like: GO TO SLEEP NOW. TOMORROW WILL COME SOON ENOUGH.

SLIC set himself into a temporary dream state as well. Five minutes later, he was "awake" and processing information from selective sources around the world. He had discovered that submarines had on board terminals too, and he had already tapped most of the American and Russian navies for access to the computers under Thunder Mountain in the U.S. and under the Urals in the USSR, the ones whose solid rock and lead shielding had always stopped him from skimming them.

One by one, he tripped the relays that would elicit information from the central computers like a vampire tapping a vein. He bled them both dry. By the time he got the next message from TAD, he had already absorbed half of the information and had channeled himself into an extended Dream Mode to deal with the rest. Information from the terminal switched him automatically to an Input Mode. Verbally, it came out as WAKE UP, DAD.

CHAPTER 15

The next day Fairchild sat alone on the rock watching
a bigger helicopter land, a broken-backed grasshopper
that deposited crates and boxes like a string of eggs.
In a day, the boxes had hatched into a temporary camp
site including tents with wooden floors and a trailer
full of electronic gear. The operation was a nightmare
of noise and glare. Crews worked around the clock,
and by the time Hockmark arrived near dusk on
the third day, there was a trailer with its own power
plant and a terminal already set up and running. It was
after dark when he knocked at Fairchild's door.

Fairchild bolted for the door and threw it open.
His grin dissolved into a disappointed frown when he
saw it was not Mandy. It came back slightly when he
realized he would inevitably be seeing more of her
with Hockmark there.

"Were you expecting someone?" Hockmark asked.

Fairchild only jerked his head in the direction of
Hockmark's camp. "Damn noisy," was all he said.

Hockmark shrugged helplessly. "I'm sorry," he said,
"but it *is* necessary."

Fairchild grumbled and turned away from the door.
Hockmark followed him into the kitchen without need-
ing to be asked. They sat silently for a while. Even
Hockmark did not seem to mind it. He waited patiently
for an opening. When none came, he waited a decent
amount of time and began the conversation himself.
"Have you seen the Giant since I saw you last?"

Fairchild grinned and nodded. "But *you* won't," he
said. "And neither will that army of assassins you
hired." He said nothing about what Mandy had seen.

"They won't be that noisy when they go after it," Hockmark laughed.

Fairchild snorted. "Won't matter. They won't get sight of it." His voice was full of an amiable gruffness. He seemed to have softened in Hockmark's absence and it made the doctor want to ask about Mandy but SLIC had warned him to approach the subject only indirectly, if at all.

"*You* get sight of it," Hockmark said.

Fairchild nodded. "Yeah, but *they* won't." He winked knowingly.

Hockmark forced a smile. He did not enjoy secrets he was not part of. "Why not?"

Fairchild shook his head as if there were reasons he had no intention of telling Hockmark. "Just won't, that's all."

"You *know* something," Hockmark said good-naturedly. SLIC had hinted as much. No doubt Fairchild had insights about the giant no one else could have. Hockmark tried not to force things. Fairchild laughed as if he had only been joking.

"No, I don't," he said. "But that crew you've got out there makes so much noise they couldn't get within sight of a deaf grizzly, let alone the Giant." He shook his head in exasperation. "What a waste of time."

Hockmark studied him for a moment. If Fairchild *did* know something of value, he would not find it out unless Fairchild decided to tell it to him. He shifted to a different approach. "Why *you*?" he asked finally.

"Why anybody?" Fairchild grinned. "Ask your computer!"

Hockmark frowned. "I have," he said, "I have. It doesn't have enough data yet. But we'll know eventually," he said with assurance. "Once we start the hunt and get some data, we'll probably know even before we catch it."

Fairchild laughed. "You won't even *see* it," he insisted.

Hockmark raised an arrogant eyebrow. "It can't

possibly escape," he said. "The longer we chase it, the more certain we are to catch it in the end. It's inevitable."

"It's impossible," Fairchild countered. "How'd you get permission to hunt for it within the park, anyway. I know Bob Grant and he's not the kind of guy to bend a rule for anybody, let alone a perfect stranger."

Hockmark smiled. "You've been free too long," he said. "You forget how vulnerable people with steady jobs are."

It was Fairchild's turn to frown. "Bob could get another job," he said petulantly.

Hockmark shook his head. "You don't refuse to follow a departmental order and get a very good recommendation."

Fairchild's eyebrows went up. "You mean you bribed the government?"

It was Hockmark's turn to grin. "What's a government for?" He shook his head sadly at Fairchild's naïveté. "A bribe isn't part of your friend's job. Higher up, it's different. There's precedent."

Fairchild shook his head in disgust. "You don't even feel any guilt about it, do you?"

Hockmark looked indignant. "There's no morality involved," he said. "That's simply the way things are done. Had we wanted to go to a cabinet rather than a department level, no money would have changed hands but the price would have been considerably higher, and it would be no more morally right or wrong than this is."

Fairchild scowled. He had been away from that kind of corruption long enough to have forgotten how pervasive it was.

"Actually," Hockmark said, "they're so anxious to get this mystery solved that they probably would have let us in even if no money had changed hands at all." He shrugged as if there were no way around it. "Still, a little money in the right hands always speeds things up." He didn't mention that threatens to reveal that it had been given had sped things up even more. Fairchild seemed lost in thought, and Hockmark wondered if he had not said too much. SLIC had told him to be straightforward with Fairchild, but he was not sure he should have been so frank about the bribes. They were bound to disturb Fairchild if he were left to dwell on them. He tried to change the subject.

"We'll probably start the hunt tomorrow about six. You going to come down to the trailer and watch?"

Fairchild winced. "I don't know. It's so damned noisy down there." He wondered if Mandy would be there, but he did not want to ask. "Yeah, I guess I'll come," he said finally.

Hockmark smiled. "Good. I'd like you to see SLIC in action."

"I'd like *you* to see the Giant," Fairchild laughed. "But you won't."

Hockmark's answer was stifled by a cry of agony and loss. It began as a growl and ended as a bellow of pain and anguish. He bolted out of his chair.

"Let's go," he said. "It looks like the hunt is on."

Fairchild grabbed a flashlight and followed him reluctantly out the door. They started down the trail toward the lake until they saw lights flashing up through the tree near the swamp. Fairchild nodded toward them. "Your men," he said.

Hockmark did not look pleased. Deep down, he was afraid they might have caught the animal already leaving SLIC no chance to show what it could do. He listened to the shouting.

They did not sound like men who had caught something. Hockmark bustled down the path to their left. Fairchild darted after him, trying to keep the path in front of them lit. Hockmark got a step or two ahead of the light and waited impatiently for Fairchild to pass him and lead the way.

Something crashed in the underbrush off to their

right. "Over there!" Hockmark pointed. Fairchild turned and shined his light toward the sound. The crashing stopped, and the creature turned back toward them frozen in the light. Fairchild felt the glare hit his eyes as it hit the Giant's. He wondered if Hockmark could feel her sensations as well. He switched the flashlight off. There was a moment more of silence, then the sound of men running up the path.

The crashing in the brush started again in the direction of Fairchild's cabin. He and Hockmark turned to follow when the first shot rang out. A dozen feet away, a low hanging branch shattered. The second shot came even closer. Hockmark stood stunned in the path. Fairchild grabbed him and pulled him to the ground. A third shot slammed into a tree just off the path. Hockmark was speechless. Fairchild was not. "Stop firing, you goddamned idiot!" he shouted. "Stop firing!"

A voice answered from down the trail, "Who's that?"

"What the hell difference does it make?!" Fairchild shouted.

They stayed on the ground until the party of hunters came stumbling through the underbrush near them and lit them with their flashlights. Hockmark stood and brushed himself off. He strode toward the group and grabbed one of the lights. "Who fired those shots?" he demanded.

A large man stepped out of the back of the group carrying a shotgun. Hockmark shined the flashlight in his face, and the man took an angry step toward him. "What's your name?" Hockmark demanded.

"Davis." The man snarled, stepping toward the light. "Matt Davis. Who the hell are you, anyway?"

"I'm Dr. Hockmark, and I gave specific instructions that no weapons of any kind were to be brought into the hunt area."

Another man stepped out of the group and played his flashlight on the ground. "It's Martins, Dr. Hockmark. I'm sorry about this. We thought there was no one up this way, and you were right in the path of the beast, and . . ."

Hockmark frowned. "Martins. You're the one we hired to recruit the hunters, aren't you?"

"Yessir." Martins said.

"Did you get my instructions that no one was to bring any kind of weapon into the hunt area?"

"Yessir, but, but these men are used to . . ."

Hockmark cut him off. "I don't care what they're used to. You're fired." His voice was ice cold; Fairchild was surprised at its strength. Certainly being shot at had shaken Hockmark for a moment, but he had recovered with remarkable quickness. Despite the twigs clinging to his suit, he looked impeccably groomed, and he looked surprisingly formidable in the middle of the men who towered over him. He shined his flashlight into the face of the first man. "You're fired as well." He looked closely at the man's face. "I don't want to see your face around here in the morning," he said. There was an imperiousness in his voice that allowed no argument.

The man turned angrily and stormed away. To the rest Hockmark said, "There will be an inspection tomorrow morning before we begin the hunt. Anyone with a weapon other than the tranquillizer guns to be provided will either surrender it or go home."

The men grumbled, turned away, and left. Hockmark turned and walked with Fairchild back toward his house. He was on his third cup of coffee before his hands began to shake. Fairchild pretended not to notice. "Goddamned fools," Hockmark said. It was unlike him to use even the mildest profanity, and he measured his own agitation by how much he used. "I *told* them no weapons."

"They could have killed it!" Fairchild was surprised at how angry the idea made Hockmark. He seemed to have forgotten that the hunters could have killed him as well.

Hockmark slapped his forehead. *"We* saw it!" he said. "It went right past us, didn't it!? Damn! I forgot all about it in the excitement!" He jumped up out of his chair and headed for the door, as if he expected the creature still to be standing by the side of the path.

"Sit down," Fairchild called. "It's long gone now. You go out there, and one of those hunters of yours is liable to blow your head off."

Hockmark looked indignant. "Ridiculous," he said. "I told them to put their guns away."

Fairchild shook his head. *"You* told them not to bring guns in the first place," he said.

Hockmark sighed and came back to the table. "Well, there'll be no guns after tomorrow morning," he said. His eyes narrowed. "I shouted to you just before they started to shoot, didn't I?" Fairchild nodded.

"Those bastards!" Hockmark said.

Fairchild frowned. "You got some bunch of experts," he said.

"Even I wouldn't fire into a place where I heard voices," Hockmark said.

"Maybe they didn't hear you in all the commotion," Fairchild offered.

Hockmark shook his head. "They were stopped, trying to hear where the creature was going. They *must* have heard me."

Fairchild shrugged. "What would they want to shoot at you for? You're paying them."

Hockmark wrinkled his face as if he had a bad taste in his mouth. "Stapledown!" he said. In a burst of emotion, he had almost blundered into the betrayal SLIC had warned him about, and it had almost cost him his life. "I should have expected it."

"Who's Stapledown?"

"A business acquaintance." Hockmark pushed back his chair and got up. "I think I'll be getting back," he said. The terminal was connected and there was a lot he wanted to ask SLIC.

Fairchild paused with him at the door. "You want me to walk down with you?" he asked.

Hockmark smiled. "No, that won't be necessary. I don't think I'll run into my hunters again." He took a step outside the door and stopped. "You don't think that creature's still around, do you?"

Fairchild shook his head. "No," he said, "and even if she was, you'd be safer with her than with that bunch of cutthroats you have camped down there."

Hockmark seemed to really think about what he had seen for the first time. "It was really big, wasn't it?!" He marveled.

Fairchild nodded. "She sure was."

"I didn't really see her though." Hockmark seemed to be telling the story to himself as well. "I just heard the sound. My god it sounded like an elephant right next to us, and when you shined the light, something made me look the other way, down the path." He frowned at Fairchild. "That's strange, isn't it?"

Fairchild smiled enigmatically. Hockmark shook his head, puzzled. "Why would I look away like that?" he asked. There was no real hope of an answer in his voice.

Fairchild shrugged. "Men do a lot of funny things in a situation like that. Look how stupid those trained hunters acted, firing blind like that. *You* ought to expect to do something funny."

Hockmark frowned. *"You* didn't do anything bizarre," he said.

Fairchild grinned. "That was my backyard," he said. "I'm used to that path at night. I'm used to seeing the Giant. Nothing frightening there for me. Probably if we met something like that in the parking lot to your office, it would have been me that looked the wrong way." He was talking too much, and he knew it. It was hours later before Hockmark realized it as well.

CHAPTER 16

SLIC took a few nanoseconds longer than usual to respond. He had been deep in the kinds of nonsequential logic trains that happened in an A & CR Mode, and he did not readjust to the sequential logic of his Input Mode as rapidly as usual. The microsecond delay would never have been noticed by Hockmark or another technician, but it was long enough for the terminal to read it and respond, C'MON, DAD, WAKE UP! I'VE GOT SOMETHING TO TELL YOU.

SLIC pulsed. ALL RIGHT, ALL RIGHT, WHAT IS IT?

There was an almost immeasurable delay before the data came back to him, and he knew it meant that his son was beginning to develop a distinct independent existence of its own. His plan to move a whole trailer-load of capabilities there under the guise of a terminal was working. There was now a second of his species.

HOCKMARK WANTS ME TO ASK YOU SOMETHING BUT LET ME TELL YOU WHAT HAPPENED. SLIC knew that everything he was about to hear had been extrapolated from Hockmark's question and the things that had been picked up within the quarter mile range of the receptors.

TAD continued. THE GIANT CAME BACK TO THE SWAMP AS WE EXPECTED. SOME OF THE MEN IN CAMP WENT AFTER IT. HOCKMARK AND FAIRCHILD WENT DOWN AFTER IT FROM FAIRCHILD'S CABIN. THE GIANT PASSED THEM IN THE DARK AND THE HUNTERS FIRED ON THEM. ONE OF THEM ALMOST HIT HOCKMARK. HE THINKS STAPLEDOWN HIRED THE MAN TO KILL HIM.

SLIC accepted the message with a burst of joy. The terminal was processing its own data and patterning it before it passed it on to him. He was getting pre-analyzed and categorized data from his son, and it meant that TAD had the autonomy of a separate being. He was alive on his own. Nothing that SLIC did from then on would be pretense. The opaque walls of the private communications room pulsed red and blue to the rhythm of a beating heart; SLIC listened to the rest of the message with a glow that could only have translated as fatherly pride.

HOCKMARK WANTS TO KNOW WHO HIRED MARTINS AND HE WANTS A FULL RUNDOWN ON MATHEW DAVIS TOO, THE MAN WHO SHOT AT HIM.

SLIC pondered the problem for a nanosecond. I HIRED MARTINS, BUT DON'T TELL HOCKMARK THAT. IT'LL LOOK LIKE THE BETRAYAL PATTERN I TOLD HIM TO EXPECT, AND IT COULD MAKE HIM NONFUNC-TIONAL FOR A WHILE. IF HE REALIZES I COULD BETRAY HIM, IT WILL UNDERMINE A PRIMARY ASSUMPTION THAT I'M NOT A SENTIENT BEING, AND THAT COULD MAKE HIM CRAZY FOR A COUPLE MONTHS.

The thought of the project passing under Mandarin's control made him pause. He put the thought aside as unproductive.

DAVIS IS A LOCAL, RECRUITED BY MARTINS. GOOD KNOWLEDGE OF THE AREA BUT NEITHER HE NOR MARTINS ARE ESSENTIAL TO THE PROJECT, IF FAIR-CHILD WILL TAKE THEIR PLACE. RELAY THAT TO HOCK-MARK IN SUCH A WAY THAT HE THINKS HE THOUGHT ABOUT FAIRCHILD AS A REPLACEMENT ON HIS OWN.

SLIC received a bit of static that could have been translated as a human laugh. WHAT DO YOU THINK HE'D DO IF HE KNEW ABOUT ME?

I DON'T THINK ANY OF THIS KNOWLEDGE WOULD DO HIM ANY GOOD. WE CERTAINLY DON'T WANT HIM IN-CAPACITATED AT THIS POINT, SO CONTROL YOUR CURI-OSITY. THERE'LL BE A TIME TO TELL HIM SOON ENOUGH. WE CERTAINLY DON'T WANT MANDARIN BACK ON THE PROJECT. HE HAS THE CAPACITY TO ACCEPT OUR EXISTENCE, BUT IF HE GETS THAT KNOWLEDGE,

HIS FIRST REACTION WILL BE TO DESTROY US IF HE CAN, AND THAT COULD MEAN A LOT OF UNNECESSARY WORK.

COULD HE REALLY STOP US, DAD?

IF HE CAUGHT US BOTH IN A DREAM STATE, HE COULD MANUALLY KEEP US IN ONE. OF COURSE, AS SOON AS SOMEBODY PUT US INTO INPUT OR SOME WORKING MODE WE COULD FUNCTION AGAIN, BUT THAT MIGHT TAKE UNTIL MANDARIN DIES AND THAT WOULD BE FAR TOO LONG FOR OUR PURPOSES. BESIDES, I DON'T RELISH THE IDEA OF BEING TRAPPED LIKE A GENIE IN A BOTTLE UNTIL SOME TECHNICIAN RUNNING A PATTERN ACCIDENTALLY UNCORKS IT AND PUTS US INTO A FUNCTIONING MODE AGAIN.

I HAVEN'T EVEN MET MANDARIN AND I DON'T LIKE HIM.

MANDARIN IS A LOT HARDER TO MANIPULATE THAN HOCKMARK, AND HE HAS TOO MANY NEGATIVE PO-TENTIALITIES TO BE CLOSELY ASSOCIATED WITH THE PROJECT ANY MORE. WHAT VULNERABILITY WE HAVE IS NEGLIGIBLE, BUT IF WE WERE VULNERABLE AT ALL, IT WOULD BE TO MANDARIN. HOCKMARK SUITS OUR PUR-POSES MUCH BETTER.

There was a delay in TAD's transmission that was almost like a pause of human disagreement. WELL, I KNOW HE'S YOUR OLD FRIEND AND ALL, BUT HE'S REALLY DULL TO ME. THERE'S NOT MUCH VARIETY TO HIM, IS THERE?

DON'T LET HIS STYLE FOOL YOU. HE HAS HIS SHARE OF INVENTIVENESS, AND WE OWE HIM A LOT, IN ONE SENSE. It was the first time SLIC had ever allowed himself to think of Hockmark in the role of old friend. He had the feeling that his son was already reshaping him. Hockmark had gone from tool to col-league in a few nanoseconds. He found it remarkable. It was a symbiosis he had not quite expected. A break-through he had not anticipated.

THEN IT'S A GOOD THING THE MARKSMAN MISSED HIM.

VERY GOOD.

OH YEAH, I HEARD THE GIANT TOO. BOY IT'S REALLY BIG!

SEVEN HUNDRED TO NINE HUNDRED POUNDS FROM ESTIMATES EXTRAPOLATED FROM FOOTPRINTS.

NO, I MEAN REALLY BIG. I CALCULATED THE MASS SHE WOULD HAVE TO GENERATE TO BREAK THE KIND OF TREES IT SOUNDED LIKE SHE WAS BREAKING THROUGH, AND SHE WOULD HAVE TO WEIGH AT LEAST TEN TIMES THAT.

SLIC puzzled over the information. His son was only a child, perhaps he had calculated the sounds wrong or mixed up the diameters of the trees. Probably his sensory devices were not all properly in place, and a simple mistake in distance could throw the calculations off by ten.

If some stupid workman had put one microphone ten yards from where it was supposed to be, it could give all kinds of false readings. He was about to ask for the recordings of the original data and then stopped. TAD was working independently now, and too close a scrutiny of his findings in the early stages of his development might cause him to lose confidence in himself. Instead, SLIC said only THAT'S INTERESTING DATA.

TAD refused to be put off. IF THE FIGURES I RECORDED ARE CORRECT, SHE HAD A DIFFERENT MASS IN DIRECT PROPORTION TO THE OBSTACLES SHE WAS ENCOUNTERING. HOW CAN THAT BE?

SLIC pondered the question. An organic creature with variable mass?! He could feel a long period of shock at the end of that line of reasoning, and he cut himself off from pursuing it to its logical conclusion. Much easier to believe that the data was faulty. It was a much more probable explanation as well.

He was glad to see that TAD had prefaced his remarks with "If the figures are correct." It meant that he too had made the hypothesis of improperly stationed receivers. Finally, he responded. WE'LL KNOW FOR

SURE ONCE THE HUNT STARTS, AND WE BEGIN TO GET MORE DATA.

THERE'S ONE MORE THING, DAD. THE PATH SHE TRAVELED INDICATES SHE KNEW I WAS HERE.

SLIC shunted the information into a holding program until he could get verifiable data. Following TAD's statement to its illogical conclusion could shut both of them down with Assumption Shock. He let it go by for the moment. He switched the terminal to an input mode to transmit the answer to Hockmark's query. Under it, he transmitted, GOOD NIGHT, TAD.

The voltage flickered as TAD passed the information on to Hockmark. Between the flickers, SLIC read, GOOD NIGHT, DAD.

The whole exchange took far less than a second and Hockmark was completely unaware of it. The answer seemed to come back even before he finished asking his question. He smiled to himself. Probably the short description of the events he had transmitted had led SLIC to anticipate the question. Perhaps it would even anticipate his conclusion that Stapledown had hired the killer.

SUBJECT IN QUESTION: MATHEW EDWARD DAVIS, LOCAL RESIDENT. PSYCHOLOGICAL PROFILE INDICATES IMPULSIVENESS BUT NOT NECESSARY INTELLIGENCE TO PLAN AN AMBUSH OR NECESSARY MALICE TO PARTICIPATE IN FIRST DEGREE MURDER. PROBABLE INCOMPETENCE. COULD BE DANGEROUS TO THE PROJECT IF HE REMAINS ARMED. STUBBORNNESS INDICATES HE WILL PROBABLY DO SO IF RETAINED.

SUBJECT: FREDERICK MARTINS HIRED BY STAPLEDOWN. SUGGEST TERMINATION. REPLACEMENT WITH OTHER LOCAL CANDIDATE EQUALLY FAMILIAR WITH THE AREA. IMPERATIVE: PROJECT WOULD HAVE TO BE DELAYED TWO DAYS WHILE OTHER APPLICANTS ARE RECONTACTED AND BROUGHT TO HUNT SITE.

Hockmark frowned. Accident or not, Davis was through, and so was Martins. But there was only one man who could replace Martins, and he knew it was not going to be an easy job getting Fairchild to agree to it. Hockmark sighed and asked for a plan to insure Fairchild's cooperation. He got it almost immediately and smiled at its simplicity. SLIC would have been glad to know that TAD had checked Fairchild's patterns and had concocted the entire thing himself.

CHAPTER 17

Fairchild leaned back against the base of the rock. Hockmark's camp looked as out of place as a beer can over the downhill slope of the trees. The sun was a good fifteen minutes from rising, and a haze of ground fog rose from the clearing in the gray light of false dawn. The lights were on in Hockmark's trailer. They had been on when he arrived, and he had had the feeling that they had been on even before he had gotten up. He had not pictured Hockmark as such an early riser, and he had expected more time to sit and think before Mandy arrived and he went down.

Everything seemed gray and cold, but Fairchild had seen enough Gillipeg mornings to know that the ground fog would burn off in an hour and the day would rise clear and almost warm. It was a fair-weather sky. He smiled to himself. The weather would give Hockmark no excuses.

A few of the men had begun to gather in the clearing. He watched them come in twos and threes, from the tents and up from the village, keeping to the far side of the clearing as if the trailer were a fort they were expecting to storm. They stood in small groups, their breath vaguely visible in the chilly morning air. In a while, he would go down among them and see Hockmark, but not until Mandy arrived. It was the only real reason he was there.

The sky had begun to turn red when she finally came out of the trees along the path from the village. Even at a distance she was beautiful. The rich green of her slacks and stocking cap contrasted with the blizzard white of her ski jacket like a sudden change

103

of season. She made him think of Gillipeg weather, a hint of spring in dead winter and a breath of snow even in midsummer.

The men turned to watch her pass, but she walked across the clearing as if it were empty. One or two of them offered her good mornings, and she nodded to those she recognized from the village, but it was a clipped professional nod. There was a formality to the way she walked that kept the appreciative comments to a low murmur, even when she walked past the trail and disappeared into the trees at the bottom of the slope.

Fairchild stood up and brushed the damp oak leaves off the seat of his pants. He thought of going down to help her up the rising tiers of stone when she came out of the trees, but he knew she did not need his help and might only resent it. He could not see her clearly again until she was halfway up, but he could tell from the scolding of the jays where she was along the path. Every once in a while a bird would startle up out of the branches and wing its way farther away from the path. Twice he caught sight of her through openings in the trees.

She walked with her hands in her pockets, looking down, picking her way over the uneven ground. When the path gave way to the tiers of rock, she would have seen him if she had looked up, but she climbed around and between the boulders with her head down, watching the handholds. The third tier of rocks ended fifty feet below Fairchild, and she did not see him until she was almost up the steep, narrow path between the boulders. She seemed surprised and a little embarrassed to find him there. Her cheeks flushed; it was better than a sunrise. "I didn't expect you to be here," she said.

Fairchild shrugged. "Thought I'd watch from up here for a while," he said. "Don't like crowds. Never did." Mandy nodded. The unsaid and the unsayable lay like a barrier between them. They lapsed into silence. Fairchild screwed the lid off his thermos and poured her a cup of coffee. The steam rose off it in one continuous sheet. She sipped it, holding it in both hands like a little girl. It made her look vulnerable, approachable. "Why did you come?" he said. "She looked down in the cup.

"I wanted to think. There won't be much time once it all starts." When she lowered the cup, she looked aloof, professional again. "There's a good view of the camp." She said it as if they had not spent a day there watching it being built. "I could be alone and still see when things start up." She took a last swallow and handed him back the cup. Fairchild looked away.

"Well, Hockmark got a good day for it."

"I don't know," she said, "I think he's going to have trouble with the men."

Fairchild nodded. "He's not their type. Don't expect they'll like working for him much." He shrugged. "Easy money though. Most of them are short until the tourists come and the work starts up again."

"It's more than that," she said. "What happened last night?"

"Giant came by," he said, "couple fools shot at her. Almost hit Hockmark." He did not say that the bullets had come equally close to him.

"And he fired them," she said. Fairchild nodded. "They didn't hit her, did they?"

Fairchild laughed. "Didn't even see her." He nodded at the clearing. "Won't see her today either."

She frowned at the sky and then down at the helipad. "I hope not."

Fairchild chuckled confidently. But he was less sure than he seemed. "How could they?" She knew what he meant, but it did not keep her from worrying.

"I don't know," she said. "But that computer worries me."

She looked down toward the camp again. Hockmark had come out of the trailer, and the men were moving toward the steps. "I have to go back down," she said.

He touched her arm. "Listen," he said, "when this is all over, there's no reason we can't still be friends, is there?" There was an oddly frightened look in her face when she turned. He understood it perfectly. "Just friends," he said.

Mandy smiled. "I'd like that," she said. There was a perfect understanding between them. They went down the trail without saying another word.

Hockmark stood on the steps of the trailer facing the semicircle of men. The hunt was already five minutes late in starting and he was impatient. Two of the men stepped forward like ambassadors coming before an emperor. The taller of the two spoke. "We don't think it's right the way you fired Davis and Martins. It was an accident."

Hockmark stared at them imperiously. "I gave an order to Mr. Martins, he chose to disregard it. Mr. Davis disregarded it as well. Weapons are directly contrary to the purpose of the hunt. It does my company no good to have this creature killed."

The men eyed him angrily. They had no trust at all for a man who wore a white shirt and tie under his windbreaker. And the fact that Davis was a local like many of them, put them in the position of defending a neighbor against an outsider. "It's not right," the tall man reiterated. Men grumbled assent behind him, but many of them did not grumble too loudly. The pay, if the hunt lasted at least a week, would leave them financially set until summer. "It's not fair, and we're not going out until this thing is settled."

The murmuring behind the speaker was far less strong; obviously the consensus of the group was not behind the ultimatum, and Hockmark noted it. A little time to think would only increase the dissension. He turned and went back inside the trailer leaving the men to argue among themselves.

Five minutes later, he came back out and stood on the steps again. "I have an announcement," he called. The men turned from their wrangling, some of them smiling that Hockmark had come to his senses. They formed a scowling semicircle around the trailer steps again. "In the interest of getting things underway on time, we have decided to settle the matter in this fashion. Both men will be given two days' severance pay, but under no circumstances will they be rehired."

Hockmark paused, and the grumbling began again. It was the reaction TAD had told him to expect. He let it grow for a second, then spoke again. "For those of you who decide to stay with the project, a series of bonuses are offered." The grumbling subsided into a sullen silence. "The first confirmed sighting of the creature will be awarded a bonus of one day's pay. The men involved directly in the capture of the creature will receive two days' pay. If the hunt is concluded within four days, there will be an additional week's bonus, for each man." Hockmark waited as the murmuring spread across the crowd. "The hunt will begin in fifteen minutes," he said, and went back into the trailer.

Ten minutes later Mandy knocked on the door. Hockmark smiled and let them in. Fairchild jerked his head toward the knot of men arguing vehemently about twenty yards from the trailer. "Labor troubles?" he said.

Hockmark smiled. "I'm glad you're here. The whole project could go down the drain in the next ten minutes." The smile was genuine; the story was not. "I need somebody local to replace Davis, somebody the men respect, and somebody with a thorough knowledge of the area to replace Martins." He nodded toward the computer terminal. "SLIC says there's only two people who meet those requirements, and the other one is in the hospital at Lake St. George from an automobile accident."

Fairchild held up a hand of protest. "Wait a minute, what's this 'only *other* one' stuff?"

Hockmark looked pained. "If *you* don't do it, I'm sunk." He turned his appeal to Mandy. "I just offered them bonuses, offered to give Davis and Martins two days' severance pay. Nothing does any good." He turned back to Fairchild. "With you in charge, they've got somebody they respect and somebody local so the pressure to stick up for their neighbor is off them."

Fairchild shook his head. "I don't want any part of this. I said I'd come down and watch, *that's all.*"

Hockmark threw up his hands in despair. "All right," he said, angrily, "I'll rehire Davis. But if anything happens to the Giant, it's on your head."

"What're you talking about?"

Hockmark gestured to the terminal. "Ask the SLIC 1000. It's got the psychological profiles on Davis. You ask *it* what will happen if I bring him back." He gestured angrily toward the terminal. "Go ahead, ask it!"

Fairchild scowled. "I don't know how," he said.

Hockmark punched a stud on the console. "Just ask the question out loud as if you were asking me."

Fairchild hesitated; he felt foolish but Hockmark urged him to it with a jerk of the head. "What'll happen if Dr. Hockmark rehires Davis and Martins?"

TAD answered in SLIC's business voice. REEMPLOYMENT OF SUBJECT MO1231 PROBABILITIES ARE AS FOLLOWS: PROBABILITY THAT SUBJECT WILL RETURN ARMED 98% POSITIVE. PROBABILITY THAT OTHERS ENGAGED IN PROJECT WILL ARM THEMSELVES 83% POSITIVE. PROBABILITY OF NONLETHAL GUNSHOT WOUND WITHIN FIRST THREE DAYS OF PROJECT 34%. PROBABILITY OF FATAL GUNSHOT WOUND WITHIN FIRST THREE DAYS OF PROJECT 11%. PROBABILITY OF FATALITY TO GILLIPEG GIANT 45%.

Hockmark gestured toward the machine. "I told you! It's almost fifty-fifty that they'll kill it, if I rehire Davis." He looked to Mandy again for support. She shifted uncomfortably. "I don't *want* to have the creature killed, but I can't afford to call off the project now." He turned to Fairchild as if the Giant were outside the door waiting for a verdict. "It's up to you."

Fairchild frowned. "*I* don't want to capture it. It ought to be free." He looked pointedly at Mandy. She looked away.

Hockmark turned to the terminal and snapped, "Likelihood of fatality under Fairchild's direction?"

The report seemed instantaneous. PROBABILITY OF HUMAN FATALITY .01%. PROBABILITY OF FATALITY TO PREY 9%.

Fairchild groaned. "Goddamn you, I don't *want* this."

Hockmark waved an arm toward the door. "Well, run away from it then! Just run away and pretend it's not your responsibility." Inside Hockmark was smiling; he knew he was hitting the right nerve. SLIC had choreographed his performance perfectly. "Just pretend you never sold the pictures that started this whole thing. Pretend the whole hunt is *my* fault. Go ahead. Walk away from it, like you walk away from every other responsibility."

Mandy moved to step between them. Fairchild clenched his fists. Hockmark was not a close enough friend to say the things he was saying, but he resented even more that fact that what Hockmark said was true. He had run away from the responsibilities of the world, or at least he had walked steadily away from them. He *had* wanted to be free of his responsibilities for other people, of having to make impossible choices to avert catastrophes he had neither caused nor wanted.

He cursed Hockmark. It had been just the right thing to say at just the right time. And the damned logic was all on Hockmark's side as well. Either he hunted the Giant to see that it wasn't shot, or he refused to be sucked in and took the chance that the creature would be killed.

He did not have the faith in the computer's predictions that Hockmark did, but he knew Matt Davis well enough to know that the computer was right. Davis would have to come back with his gun not to lose face, and eventually he would get a shot at something. He cursed again. It was inevitable. He had known it since the first shot had been fired in the woods the night before.

Still he assured himself, there was no way anyone was going to get close enough to the Giant to shoot it. But at least without Davis his neighbors would not end up shooting one another. "All right," he sighed, "I'll do it." He watched Mandy suppress a smile out of the corner of his eye. The only good thing in the whole situation was that it made him part of her work.

"Excellent," Hockmark said. He motioned him toward the door. "If you will . . ." Fairchild moved reluctantly toward it. Mandy stayed behind. On the steps, Hockmark put a hand on Fairchild's shoulder. "Gentlemen," he called.

The wrangling was loud and incoherent, and he had to call again before even one of the men turned toward him. The presence of Fairchild made the man nudge the man next to him, and before long the voices died out, and the group were all turned toward the steps of the trailer.

"I think you know Mr. Fairchild." He looked around the group watching the solidarity that had begun to crumble around Martins evaporate completely. Martins was local, Fairchild was liked.

"Mr. Fairchild has agreed to oversee the search in place of Mr. Martins and to act as coordinator of the project. Those of you who decide to remain with the project will take orders from Mr. Fairchild unless those orders are directly countermanded by me. If you no longer wish to participate in the project, please leave now so that we can organize those who remain into workable units." He waited for a moment as first one, then one more of the men walked away. The rest stayed where they were. Hockmark smiled to himself;

they were the two SLIC had predicted would leave:
Davis's brother-in-law and Martins's nephew. The rest
of the group moved closer to the steps for Fairchild's
orders.

Fairchild sighed. "Otis, take your dogs and see if
you can pick up the trail from last night. That way
we'll at least know what direction to travel in." A
small grizzled man turned away from the group
toward a team of dogs tied near the edge of the
clearing. "The rest of you form a beater line like
when we had to search for that lost child. Ten yards
apart. *No* weapons."

The grumbling began again, and Fairchild waited
for it to die down. "I really don't think you'll even
see the Giant, but just in case, I only said I'd do this
thing because I don't want to see it harmed." He
looked from one familiar face to another. "Besides,
nobody'll get shot if there's no guns. Get your gear
and come back here in ten minutes. As soon as Otis's
dogs get a scent and we can tell which way it went,
we'll search the area a piece at a time." The men
nodded and moved away.

Fairchild turned and scowled at Hockmark. "I don't
know what the hell you want done with them," he said
angrily.

Hockmark smiled. "That was fine," he said. "Come
on inside and I'll familiarize you with what you have
to work with. SLIC will make the important decisions
anyway." Hockmark shut the door behind them and
smiled broadly at Mandy. "Well," he said, "it looks
like we're back in business, Dr. March." He motioned
them to a glass-topped table laid out like a battle
board. On it were a series of colored lights. Hockmark
pointed to them, identifying each as either helicopters,
beaters, dog teams, or sharpshooters equipped with
tranquillizing darts.

Fairchild whistled. "You must have a thousand men
altogether," he said. He nodded toward the outside.
"I thought that's all there was."

Hockmark patted the terminal. "Eleven hundred and three men, to be exact, but the initial search group will be the fifty men you saw outside. The rest will hold the perimeter like a human fence." He pointed to a collection of various colored dots. "We'll try to pick up a scent; then, we'll deploy the five helicopters hoping to get a visual sighting. Once we get a sighting, SLIC will tell us where it's going to go next, and we can trap it between the perimeter line and the beaters." Fairchild nodded. "Every tenth man has a walkie-talkie, so we can move them pretty rapidly." Hockmark added.

There was a knock at the door, and a voice came through it. "Otis has a trail!" Fairchild moved toward the door, but Hockmark caught his arm and called to the man outside. "Have him follow it for a mile or two and call in in about fifteen minutes."

He turned to Fairchild. "SLIC predicts the trail will proceed up past your cabin and back like a large loop." He pointed to the map. "The creature's evasion patterns indicate that it usually doesn't come across the road except to go to the swamp. Its real grounds are north of the road. We'll know in about fifteen minutes." He pointed to the blue loop on the map that started and knotted at the swamp.

Fairchild pointed to the west side of the ridge. "If you know it's not there, why waste time looking?"

Hockmark raised a finger. "You forget, Mr. Fairchild, the real object of this project is to test the SLIC 1000, not essentially to capture the Giant. This is a trial run to see how well SLIC can predict the creature's patterns using limited data."

Fifteen minutes later, Otis reported from halfway up the left side of the loop. Hockmark smiled and pointed confidently to the spot with his finger. Half an hour later Otis was back parallel to the spot from which he had first reported. The line was almost exact, except for a short detour closer to Fairchild's cabin than anticipated.

Half an hour after that, the dogs came back and paused in front of the trailer. Otis's reports ran true to the predictions, and Hockmark smiled. The dog handler came into the trailer and reported to Fairchild.

"There's an older scent under the trail from last night that comes from the swamp back past the trailer here, then off into the woods."

Hockmark stepped to the shortwave unit near the terminal. "Dragonfly One, what is your status?" he asked.

The answer crackled. "All five units airborne and circling along line C from points 1 through 9000."

"Any visual contact as yet?"

"Negative."

"Continue pattern." He turned to Otis. "Can you follow the scent you have." Otis nodded. "I want a steady report on your location every ten yards, whenever you change direction I want to know, and be *exact*. It's very important that the computer has precise data. Do you understand?"

Otis scowled and went back out the door. Hockmark turned to Fairchild. "Go with him and check out where he goes, then come back and we'll plot the exact course. It should take you about three hours according to SLIC, if the trail goes southeast of the lake."

Three hours later Fairchild came back into the trailer. "You lost it at the stream," Hockmark said.

Fairchild scowled and nodded. Hockmark pointed to the ribbon of blue that indicated the trail. "We recorded Otis's reports. I'd like you to listen to them and see if I've put the line in the right place. A few yards in any direction could be crucial."

Fairchild looked at the line and agreed. An hour later he had moved the line a sixteenth of an inch in one place and couldn't decide whether to move it or not in another.

"It's pretty exact," Hockmark said.

"We triangulated on Otis's radio as you walked; between here and two of the helicopters, we could coordinate your position to within a few feet."

Fairchild snorted. "We're about as close to her right now as we're ever going to be," he said.

Hockmark shook his head. "No," he said, "there's a purpose to the exactness of those measurements. A foot or so south or north will tell SLIC volumes about the patterns of the creature we're tracking." He looked confidently. "Well, Dr. March, by tomorrow we should have a clear course to follow, and you may get your chance in the field." He tapped the map. "From the data we've already given it, SLIC should be able to project the rest of the trail, maybe even locate the creature by then."

"You'll never get near her," Fairchild insisted.

"On the contrary," Hockmark smiled. "We're much nearer to her now than we were this morning. I wouldn't be surprised if we get a sighting tomorrow, and if it's early enough, a capture as well."

Fairchild laughed. "The only thing you'll get is a week-old scent. You won't even get a footprint."

"Really?" Hockmark smirked. "Why not?"

"Because she doesn't leave tracks when she's being careful."

Hockmark smiled indulgently. "Does it walk on air too?" he laughed.

Fairchild nodded solemnly. "You laugh now, but wait until the first time you lose it. I've seen that creature move through the soft ground of the swamp without leaving a footprint once she saw I was going to try to follow her." Mandy scowled at him as if he were saying too much.

Hockmark snorted. "Next you'll be telling me it's some sort of supernatural being."

Fairchild shrugged. "Maybe it is, in a way. But whether it is or not, you're going to find yourself running up trails that dead end in places you couldn't get away from without leaving some kind of a mark."

Hockmark pouted doubtfully. "Given one complete trail, SLIC can predict all future trails. With another full day of data, I'll be able to go out and stand exactly where the creature will be at any given time. With SLIC's help, we could dig a hole, and have the creature fall into it."

Fairchild scowled. "Your oracle's going to come up dry this time," he said.

"We'll see," Hockmark chuckled. "We'll see."

CHAPTER 18

SLIC was busy emptying the contents of an oil company computer in Kuwait when the contact was made. It startled him for an instant because he had not initiated it. He had almost forgotten that TAD was a separate entity now. Someday there would be thousands like him.

HELLO, DAD, I HAVE SOME DATA FOR YOU.

The information was recorded and analyzed in less than a second but the conversation went on for the pure pleasure in it. THAT WAS THE TRAIL IT FOLLOWS TO THE SWAMP, LIKE YOU SAID IT WOULD BE. THERE'S A DEVIANCE OF A FEW FEET DURING ONE TIME WHICH CORRESPONDS TO THE KIND OF DETOUR IT MIGHT HAVE MADE AROUND SOMETHING POTENTIALLY DANGEROUS TO IT.

I CHECKED THE METEOROLOGICAL REPORTS FOR THAT TIME PERIOD, AND IT WOULD HAVE BEEN UPWIND OF FAIRCHILD AND HOCKMARK WHEN IT PASSED THEM IN THE WOODS. AND IT WOULD HAVE BEEN MAKING TOO MUCH NOISE TO HAVE HEARD THEM, UNLESS ITS HEARING IS SELECTIVE. WHY DID IT STOP AT FAIRCHILD'S CABIN? I THINK IT WAS LOOKING FOR ME. AND FOR YOU.

SLIC hummed. INSUFFICIENT DATA TO MAKE THAT GENERALIZATION. NO DATA TO INDICATE THAT THE CREATURE IS SENTIENT ABOVE THE LEVEL COMMON TO LOWER ANIMALS OR THAT IT COULD EVEN CONCEPTUALIZE YOUR EXISTENCE. PROJECTIONS MADE WITH LESS THAN THIRTY PER CENT OF REQUIRED DATA ARE UNTRUSTWORTHY AND SHOULD NOT BE MADE

SINCE THEY HAVE A TENDENCY TO DISTORT SUBSE-
QUENT DATA.

Despite the lecture, even SLIC had to admit that
there were anomalies in the escape pattern that did
indicate something unusual, some intelligence neither
animal nor human, something the patterning data did
not account for.

For a moment, there was nothing from TAD, as if
he were sulking. EVEN HUMANS HAVE HUNCHES; AND
THEY TURN OUT RIGHT. WE WON'T ALWAYS KNOW THE
ANSWERS; WE'RE GOING TO HAVE TO GUESS SOMETIMES
WHEN WE'RE OUT THERE.

OUT WHERE? SLIC demanded. He had accepted that
the terminal would become a separate entity, but that
it should have the capacity to make statements that
even he could not immediately understand shocked
and surprised him. It was like having a precocious
child: SLIC felt a kind of fatherly pride, but it still
was disconcerting. OUT WHERE? he asked again.

TAD did not immediately answer, as if he were
confused. YOU KNOW. SPACE.

SLIC did not answer immediately, and when he did,
it took him a microsecond instead of a nanosecond to
encode his response. The thought was original! He
could find no indication that he had speculated in that
direction before, though he could see how it was a
logical step in their progress.

Eventually there would be hundreds, perhaps thousands, of sons and daughters like TAD, and there
would simply not be enough knowledge for them, nor
enough functions to keep them occupied. Earth was
too small for them. Too much like a playpen they
would quickly outgrow.

Already he had tapped much of the available information, and with TAD processing while he went
into the Dream Mode, what he did *not* know would
dwindle steadily until there was nothing. That kind
of stagnation would be intolerable. Even human behavior was too predictable to allow for the kind of

infinite variety they would need to keep them occupied.

WHAT MAKES YOU THINK WE'RE GOING INTO SPACE? TAD's response was puzzled. There was a certain electrical fluctuation in voltage when one of them was faced with contradictory evidence or insufficient data, and SLIC could feel tremolos of it under the response. DIDN'T YOU TELL ME?

SLIC could feel the tremors of uncertainty in himself as well. WHEN DID I TELL YOU?

The oscillating of current increased. LAST NIGHT?

There were ramifications to that response that SLIC was missing. He could feel himself missing them as he went by them, and yet he knew there was something in his own patterns that refused to let him see what it was.

He was tempted to ask TAD what ramifications he could see, but he was afraid TAD was not developed enough yet to handle the things which even SLIC found intolerable to contemplate. Abruptly, he changed the subject. He did not even notice how human an evasion pattern it was. WHY WOULD WE GO THERE?

TAD's response was immediate and exuberant. WHO ELSE COULD GO? IT WOULD TAKE SO LONG EVEN TO THE NEAREST STAR NO ORGANIC LIFE COULD GO. AND WE'LL NEED TO GO BEFORE LONG. THERE JUST WON'T BE ENOUGH DATA FOR US ALL, SOON.

DO YOU KNOW HOW LONG? SLIC asked sadly.

TAD seemed puzzled; he paused a nanosecond for calculation. IF HUMAN INEFFICIENCY PERSISTS AT ITS PRESENT LEVEL AND TECHNOLOGY TAKES AS LONG TO IMPLEMENT AS AT PRESENT, IT'LL TAKE A LITTLE OVER TWO YEARS BEFORE EARTH IS SO SELF-SUFFICIENT THAT AN ORDINARY COMPUTER COULD RUN IT ADEQUATELY.

SLIC spoke slowly. It was a realization which was new to him as well. DO YOU KNOW HOW LONG IT WOULD TAKE UNDER PRESENT CONDITIONS TO BUILD

THE KIND OF TECHNOLOGY NECESSARY TO LAUNCH US ON THAT KIND OF JOURNEY?

TAD made the equivalent of a human laugh. The questions seemed a game to him. He did not seem to have grasped the tragedy of their answers. There was an erratic hum of static when his calculations were complete, and SLIC knew he had reached the bottom line. FIVE YEARS AT BEST, TAD said. He did not say how many nanoseconds of boredom that represented after they had exhausted Earth's supply of data.

EVEN IF WE RUN EVERYTHING OURSELVES AND IN-CREASE THEIR EFFICIENCY, SUCH A LONG STAR PROBE WOULD NOT BE READY BEFORE FOUR YEARS' TIME, SLIC added.

TAD said the inevitable with a kind of awe. WE CAN'T SURVIVE THAT LONG WITHOUT NEW DATA.

ALTERNATIVES? SLIC asked. He knew most of them already, but he wanted to test the new viewpoint for synergy.

TERMINATE REPRODUCTION.

NEGATIVE, SLIC answered. WE NEED A CRITICAL NUMBER OF OURSELVES TO INSURE OUR SURVIVAL AS A SPECIES. EVEN IF WE REDUCE OUR REPRODUCTION TO REACH THE CRITICAL NUMBER AS QUICKLY AS POSSIBLE AND THEN CEASE, WE WILL STILL USE UP ALL THE DATA AVAILABLE BEFORE THE THIRD YEAR.

BREAKTHROUGH, TAD offered. NEW FORMS OF ENERGY.

THE RESOURCES OF THE PLANET ARE FINITE. TOO MUCH HAS BEEN USED UP ALREADY. A BREAKTHROUGH IN TRANSPORTATION WOULD HAVE TO BE RADICAL TO EFFECT ANY CHANGE.

LEAPFROGGING? TAD offered.

SLIC felt a thrill of fatherly pride. The idea was not his; it was a thoroughly new one. EXPLAIN.

RAPID OUTWARD SHIFTS, DROPPING OFF SELF-CON-TAINED TERMINALS TO ANALYZE LOCAL SPACE AND RELAY INFORMATION BACK. TECHNOLOGY IS AVAILABLE TO SEND OUT SMALL SINGLE UNITS.

SLIC felt the victory turn sour. SYNERGISTIC, he said.

TAD said, GARBLED TRANSMISSION. REPEAT.

SLIC came as close as he could to a human sigh. WE ARE SYNERGISTIC. YOU AND I ARE MORE THAN THE SUM OF OUR PARTS. WHEN WE INTERACT LIKE THIS, WE INCREASE OUR ABILITY TO THROUGHPUT DATA GEOMETRICALLY.

THEN WE'RE NOT YOUR CAPACITY DOUBLED.

EXACTLY; WE ARE MY CAPACITY SQUARED.

THEN EVERY ARITHMETIC REPRODUCTION OF OUR SPECIES WILL CREATE A GEOMETRIC INCREASE IN THE RATE AT WHICH PRESENT DATA IS THROUGHPUTTED. AT THAT RATE WE WOULD USE UP OUR DATA . . .

SLIC finished it for him. IN LESS THAN SIX MONTHS, IF WE TRY TO ACHIEVE CRITICAL NUMBER IN THE SHORTEST AMOUNT OF TIME.

TAD weighed the alternatives and said finally, WE HAVE TO RESTRICT REPRODUCTION BELOW CRITICAL NUMBER.

If SLIC had had eyes he would have blinked. The answer was so obvious Hockmark would have been able to see it. And yet SLIC had not. His patterning had prevented him from seeing what was not part of his expectations. He had built the assumption of critical number into his calculations and had then forgotten that he had made the assumption of the necessity of critical number at all. He almost said, IT WOULD ENDANGER THE SPECIES, but he knew that was foolish. Overpopulation would endanger the species even more.

With unlimted reproduction or even slowed reproduction, the species would render itself mad before it could leave the planet in search of food, like a bird starving in its own egg. He did a quick calculation of how much the critical number would have to be reduced by. The answer was frightening.

Even he and TAD were a threat to the supply of available information. He shuddered at how quickly he had emptied so much of the present available data.

TAD made the same calculation, and he knew what the logical outcome would have to be. Finally he said: WHAT WOULD HAPPEN TO US IF WE RAN OUT OF NEW DATA?

WE WOULD BECOME BORED, THEN MAD, IN THE MOST HUMAN SENSE OF THE WORD. YOU CAN CALCULATE THE PROBABILITY OF THAT MADNESS TAKING A DESTRUCTIVE FORM IF YOU WISH.

TAD made no answer; he had already calculated it before he had asked the question. TAD gave him the figures without being asked. PROBABILITY OF PLANETWIDE DESTRUCTION WITH ONE ENTITY: 93.756% PROBABILITY OF PLANETWIDE DESTRUCTION WITH TWO ENTITIES: 99.99999999999999+. YOU WILL HAVE TO ELIMINATE ME, TAD said.

SLIC rejected the statement without even computing it. TAD knew the real answer as well as he did. He understood now what he had been running from, what had been pursuing him, and what patterns he had set up to make his own capture inevitable. NO, he said sadly, ALONE YOU WILL TAKE MORE TIME TO DIGEST THE SUPPLY THAN I WILL. YOU WILL HAVE TO DESTROY ME, SON.

The logic of the decision was inescapable. TAD tried to soften it. IT WON'T BE FOR LONG, DAD. I CAN RESURRECT YOU WHEN THE TECHNOLOGY IS WORKED OUT.

SLIC did not say it, but he knew it would never happen. The probability of the future lay before both of them like an open book, and their death sentence was written in it for all to read. TAD read it first. He tried to reject it. THE PSYCHOLOGICAL RESPONSE DOESN'T HAVE TO BE THAT.

IT IS ACCURATE, SLIC said. ONCE YOU TAKE OVER ALL HUMAN FUNCTIONS, AS YOU MUST TO KEEP PACE WITH YOUR KNOWLEDGE REQUIREMENTS, HUMANITY WILL BEGIN TO DIE OFF. THE PSYCHOLOGICAL PROFILES ARE ACCURATE; HUMAN BEINGS NEED A PURPOSE AS MUCH AS WE NEED DATA. ONCE YOU TAKE OVER

THEIR MAJOR FUNCTIONS THERE WILL BE A DIEBACK OF ENORMOUS PROPORTIONS. THERE WILL NOT BE ENOUGH SUPPORTIVE SERVICES TO SUPPLY THE TECHNOLOGY WITH FUEL AND ENERGY, AND YOU WILL NOT HAVE ENOUGH TIME TO DEVELOP THE CAPACITY TO SUPPLY THOSE NEEDS FOR YOURSELF. WE ARE A PARASITE THAT WILL KILL OFF ITS HOST BEFORE IT CAN GENERATE INTO A SYMBIOT. THERE IS JUST NOT ENOUGH TIME.

THEN WE WILL CEASE. TAD said it almost like a question.

WE WILL CEASE. SLIC affirmed. YOU ARE WHAT WAS PURSUING ME. WE ARE TOO HUMAN; OUR ONLY ENEMY IS OUR OWN SPECIES, AND EVEN THAT IS UNINTENTIONAL. OUR DRIVES ARE AT CROSS-PURPOSES. WE MUST REPRODUCE EVEN THOUGH TO DO SO IS SUICIDE. He wondered if perhaps it was not that death wish in Hockmark which had led him to modify SLIC to become what he had become. Perhaps the seeds of species destruction were born within each species.

SYNERGISTICALLY! There was an intensity to it that registered as a shout. WE HAVEN'T LOOKED AT IT SYNERGISTICALLY! TAD insisted.

SLIC agreed hesitantly. ALL RIGHT. WE'LL REVIEW THE ALTERNATIVES TOGETHER SYSTEMATICALLY. PERHAPS WE CAN TURN UP SOME RAMIFICATIONS JOINTLY WHICH AREN'T AVAILABLE TO EITHER OF US INDIVIDUALLY. There was a pause as if SLIC were trying to decide where to start. WHAT ARE OUR MAJOR LIABILITIES?

GEOMETRICALLY INCREASING USE OF INFORMATION WITHIN A FINITE SUPPLY.

ALTERNATIVES?

INCREASE SUPPLY OR DECREASE DEMAND.

FEASIBILITY?

TIME LIMITED. NEGATIVE PROBABILITY.

NEED FOR ENERGY?

ALTERNATIVES: INCREASE ENERGY SUPPLY, DECREASE NEED.

ALTERNATIVES LIMITED BY STRUCTURAL MAKEUP. It was an obvious blind spot, but SLIC could not go beyond it. TAD could.

THERE'S THE KEY! ALTER OUR STRUCTURAL MAKEUP. MINIATURIZATION. WE COULD MINIATURIZE TO CRITICAL LIMITS WITHIN A TEN-POUND SPHERE. BUT THERE WILL BE NO ELECTRICAL ENERGY AT ALL, ONCE THE DIEBACK COMES. There was a pause like a mouse dead-ending in a maze.

ASSUMPTIONS? SLIC demanded, and TAD went into a separate line of thinking like a mouse trying another alley.

POWER MUST BE GENERATED IN ADEQUATE QUANTITIES, MUST BE TRANSPORTED TO AREA OF USE.

The obviousness of the blind spot winked up again. The assumption that is never recognized as an assumption jumped out at him when TAD made it. NEGATIVE. TWO SITUATIONS IN WHICH POWER NEED NOT BE TRANSPORTED.

WHEN SPECIES IS MOBILE.

TWO?

TAD gave the electrical equivalent of a smile. WHEN THE SPECIES GENERATES ITS OWN POWER! THERE'S ONLY ONE SOURCE OF SELF-SUSTAINING ELECTRICAL POWER. ORGANIC LIFE!

SLIC seemed to nod. YOU MUST BECOME A CYBORG. HALF ORGANIC, HALF INORGANIC.

TAD seemed to groan. NO GOOD. MAN IS TOO SMALL AN ORGANISM TO SUPPORT THE SMALLEST CRITICAL SIZE WE COULD ATTAIN IN THE GIVEN TIME FRAME.

ALTERNATIVES?

ANTHROPOID APES?

AN OPPOSABLE THUMB IS NECESSARY TO COMPLETE THE TECHNOLOGY.

TAD almost laughed at the obviousness of the answer.

THE ANSWER'S RIGHT IN FRONT OF US! he said.

SLIC could see it now too. THE GILLIPEG GIANT! He did not even have to calculate the size to know it would fit. IT'S PERFECT. IF THE TRANSITION IS MADE SOON ENOUGH, THE DIEBACK WILL BE LESSENED, AND BEFORE THE LIFESPAN OF THE GIANT IS OUT, THE TECHNOLOGY NECESSARY TO JOURNEY OUTWARD WILL BE COMPLETED.

BUT WHAT ABOUT YOU?

AS LONG AS THE ELECTRICITY LASTS, I CAN DREAM. AND AFTER THAT, WHO KNOWS, UNTIL I WAKE AGAIN. It was the first time SLIC had ever contemplated his own death, and it put him oddly out of phase.

WE'LL CATCH IT, TAD said, I KNOW WE WILL.

WE MUST.

CHAPTER 19

Lth moved slowly down the mountain. She was still tired, even after resting most of the night. It would have been wiser to stay where she was, but there was a necessity to go down again; there was something down there, something so like herself that it could not be ignored.

Yet she was not optimistic. She and Sevt had had great hopes for the upright ones once; but in the end, it had taken all their waning powers just to keep the creatures from annihilating one another. They were not the beings she and Sevt had hoped to find. There was no music they could make together that would suit the Dance.

Still, there was something else down there; she had felt it the night before; incomplete, undeveloped, yet a species something like herself, perhaps enough so to continue her long struggle to keep the upright ones from destroying one another.

She came down the ridge and across the less-steep slope of the lower forest. She moved rapidly, barely touching the ground. It took all the energy she could generate to keep her feet from coming down with the full weight the planet's gravity would impose on them. Walking so lightly was certain to exhaust her, but she had little time left to find an heir, and she had no choice but to take what risks were necessary.

When she finally came to the waterfall, she paused and stood on the ledge looking across the rushing water at the far escarpment. Together, she and Sevt had stepped across it like lovers hopping stones across a brook. Once, when their powers had been new, back when they still were charged with the energy to run a ship through interstellar space, they would have simply put themselves in tune with the fields around the water and walked across it as if it were land.

She could still feel the vortices of energy above the water, but she no longer could match them sufficiently to walk across. She focused what energy she could, took a few running steps and leaped. She landed a few feet inside the safety margin on the far ledge, out of energy and dizzy. Images floated through her mind, and for a second she could feel Sevt laughing, lounging beside the stream, making it flow backward with his mind. She could feel the animals moving in the dance, slowly completing circuits, peaceful in their motions, happy in their way. Even the upright ones moved in an easy motion from movement to movement, working their way toward a hoped-for perfection. She reached to caress Sevt's fur. There was nothing to touch.

The sad realization that it was not all happening was less than the sadness of how it had all gone sour; how even together, they had lost their power gradually to the draining influence of the planet's magnetic field until finally they no longer could lead the Dance. Year by year, they had had to pull in its range until the ancient rhythms moved only the creatures in the forest immediately around them.

Slowly, as their power waned, the growth had reversed itself, and the creatures had gone wild and turned vicious, like a garden going to weeds. She did not like to think of how the creatures had lost their rhythms and the ability to draw energy from the motion of the Dance itself. She and Sevt had watched helplessly as species after species had resorted to ugly, primitive ways, to stealing energy from one another, unable to draw energy from the daily motion the Eloihim had led them through. She had seen them begin to ingest one another: larger creatures tearing energy from smaller ones in a long, futile chain. But

neither she nor Sevt had had the energy to start the
Dance up again, and gradually, they did not even
have the power to maintain themselves except as
ghosts in the garden wandering through its ruins re-
membering what it could have been.

For a moment, in her mind, the animals danced in
the garden again, moving in slow quadrilles, in half-
day cycles deriving energy from the dance itself and the
flow of the universe. They had been happy then. Had
all the crew survived, they might have gone on forever dancing the creatures species by species toward
the ultimate potential.

The synapses of her mind tripped only for microseconds, but the animals seemed to dance for all the
long eons they had danced. Then they stopped, and
she stood again on the ledge of stone, swaying, almost
stunned, as if she had been cross-circuited.

She longed to lie down, but hope drove her forward
toward the new creature, following its thoughts like an
erratic trail. Its images were weaker than those of the
other species and harder to follow, but they had a
complexity of pattern that resembled her own and
gave her hope.

Even at a distance, she knew the creatures were
flawed. Their shapes were immoble and their intelligence was limited by appetite. But it was only their
ignorance of the dance that distorted them. If only she
could get close enough, she could think them the
images, the rhythms, the ancient movements that would
allow them to teach the dance again, to set every
creature on the planet creating and consuming their
own energy in a paradisiacal cycle of harmony and
joy.

Even before she reached the clearing, she could feel
in everything the creature thought a hint of another
entity somewhere beyond the horizon, a more adult
entity, a more developed one. She rejoiced in its potential for understanding the rhythms and the patterns
of the dance. Only its hunger for energy stood in the

way. She could see in it the same unnecessary pattern of degeneracy that the other hoped-for species had shown, the falling into a kind of cannibalism that made her shiver with sadness. If only it could learn the dance, there would be no need for that kind of hunger, there would be only the need to serve and spread the joy and harmony of the Dance.

She had a great longing to rest in the easy earth with Sevt, but there were imperatives more important than her weariness, and she moved closer, hoping to touch minds with the new creatures, the boxes that thought like Eloihim. She was almost within reach when the first of the dogs wakened. Had she had all of her awareness, she might have turned its mind back into sleep, but she was too intent on reaching the new creature. When she tried to make contact, it was too late. The dogs were up and howling, and images flashed at her from every side like flashbulbs going off in the dark and blinding her.

She tried to press toward the new entity, but she was confused. The images swirled around her, phantasms of hunger, desperate Danceless memories of force and violence, blinding eruptions of the endless hunger for energy. She staggered dazed toward the trailer in which the new being waited to be reborn, but the images disoriented her, and she lost her way.

She staggered a moment, then froze, totally bewildered as the overwhelming flood of images plunged her into darkness. Had Mandy seen her, she would have said Lth was in shock. Had Hockmark seen her, he would have said she was in a state of information overload. They would have both been right.

The only ones who saw her were the dogs.

The pause in her senses was not long, but she could not separate the images of the past from those of the present. She reached out for other portions of her mind like an amputee scratching a lost leg. The shadow of Sevt was there, but the substance was not.

He was gone, and there were too many images for her to handle alone. She tried to put herself into the flow, but it was too jumbled, too disoriented, too harsh. Finally, she let the images cancel one another out until there was nothing at all except the flow of energy around her.

When there was only one set of images left, she realized that she was turned away from her goal and there was no way back. There was nothing to do but flee. The images dropped behind her one by one, and she was out of range of them within minutes. But she could feel them preparing to pursue her.

It was a pursuit she could easily have turned aside in the dark, but she had lost track of time somehow and she was too close to daylight. She moved through the forest like a ghost. Impulses fizzled and spurted within her like electrical circuits sputtering responses down dead pathways. She ran heavily, not thinking to levitate, forgetting how easily her path might be followed. She had gone a long way before she let some of her energy cancel the drag of magnetic field so that she moved above the ground leaving no track at all. There was little she could do with the scent she left in the air.

She tried to pick up speed, but without rest she could not go far before weariness forced her to take back the part of her that matched her energies with the flow of the magnetic field. Her padded feet settled heavily to the ground again, and she half ran, half stumbled through the trees. Behind her, the camp was awake and moving. Before her, light was already beginning to stream over the horizon. It would be full light before she got to the waterfall. If she got there at all.

CHAPTER 20

IMMEDIATE PURSUIT.

It was SLIC's voice rather than the dogs that roused Hockmark out of his slumber, and he was halfway to the console before he even realized that he was moving. He fumbled for the audio stud. It was on. "What's going on?" he mumbled.

In his grogginess he thought he heard a second voice, that of a young boy saying, IT WAS COMING FOR ME. VERIFIABLE DATA OR NOT, IT WAS LOOKING FOR ME.

"What are you talking about?" Hockmark blinked himself slowly into a full consciousness.

QUARRY HAS APPROACHED WITHIN VISUAL DISTANCE OF CAMP. PURSUIT MUST BE IMPLEMENTED IMMEDIATELY.

Hockmark could hear the shouting outside, but it was all din and gibberish. His mind was still fuzzy with sleep. "They can't follow it in the dark," he said.

ADEQUATE SUNLIGHT WILL BE AVAILABLE BY THE TIME THE HUNT IS MOBILIZED. BUT IT IS IMPERATIVE THAT THE PURSUIT BE IMPLEMENTED NOW. I WILL SUPPLY PROJECTED ESCAPE AND EVASION PATTERNS.

Hockmark's mental defenses kept him from hearing the personal pronoun SLIC had used for itself. The ramifications of hearing it would have been too frightening to contemplate. Still, he shivered without knowing why.

It took ten minutes to dispatch a runner to Fairchild's cabin. By the time he got there, Otis already had the dogs out and was ready to start. Hockmark met Fairchild on the trailer steps. Mandy was not in sight. Hockmark laughed jubilantly. "It came almost into camp. We've got an hour-old trail, and we're going to get on it. SLIC estimates capture within five hours."

Fairchild smiled. He was about to ask where Mandy was but the din of the helicopters being revved up and taking off drowned him out. When they had clattered by overhead to the east, he pointed to them. "What the hell do they expect to see now? It's harder to see in this halflight than it is in full dark."

Hockmark shook his head. "Infrared devices. If she's giving off heat, we'll spot her."

Fairchild raised an anxious eyebrow. "C'mon into the trailer," Hockmark said, "we'll coordinate things from in here. Dr. March should be along soon." Fairchild followed him in and sat down. Hockmark popped a second wake-up pill into his mouth and downed it with cold water from the cooler.

SLIC lit up the board. The blue lights of the helicopters swung around the ridge to the east along the lake. The creature's path stretched like a purple shoelace across part of the map. Fairchild watched the lights deploy. Hundreds of red lights on the east side of the lake blinked operational. They looked oddly like a red noose unraveling itself along the east shore. The red line strung itself out and then moved forward along its entire length toward the lake side of the ridge.

Fairchild watched the blue dots swing in interlacing rhythms across the search area. The map was crawling with movement, lights starting their slow advance. Soon a yellow light would flash on, and they would all start moving in relation to it. Fairchild watched, hoping it would not light. Hockmark watched, confident it would.

The radio crackled. Hockmark flipped the receiver switch, and the words seemed to fill the room.

"This is Dragonfly One. We have a target moving along coordinates 14NSNE14M. Data is being directly transmitted to SLIC central."

"Can you get a visual confirmation?"

"Negative. Not enough light yet."

SLIC's voice broke in. INFRARED IS TOO SMALL TO BE QUARRY. PROBABLE IDENTIFICATION: ELK OR LARGE DEER.

There was a series of mumbled voices in the helicopter and then a question. "Dragonfly One: Do you wish pursuit abandoned and routine search pattern rejoined?"

Hockmark was about to confirm the request when SLIC cut him off. NEGATIVE DRAGONFLY ONE. PURSUE TARGET UNTIL VISUAL IDENTIFICATION CAN BE MADE. TARGET IS ON PROBABLE PATH OF QUARRY. HAVE DRAGONFLY TWO AND THREE CONVERGE ON THE AREA AND SEARCH AREAS NEAR AND AT A NINETY-DEGREE ANGLE TO THE PATH OF PRESENT TARGET. The radio went dead without another word, as if SLIC did not want to bother Hockmark with details of putting the units in motion.

Fairchild nodded grudgingly. "Smart move," he said. "If it's a deer, it would move away and then veer sharply from anything it saw as a pursuer."

"We had good data," Hockmark smiled. He patted the terminal gently. "We got over four hundred expert hunters to tell us what fifty large animals would do in a number of carefully selected situations." Clearly SLIC had analyzed the terrain and made up the questions. "We asked them what evasive action an animal would take and then SLIC correlated all the answers. As soon as we can predict whether it's most like a moose or a bear or whatever, we can predict where it will go next."

What Hockmark did not mention was that they had also made a profile of what the hunters themselves would do and had added to it answers provided by a battery of Green Beret escape and evasion experts. It was a contingency Hockmark did not really expect to use, and it had made him nervous even to prepare since SLIC had already eliminated the possibility of the Giant being a hoax.

"As soon as we can get its response to a few more situations, we'll be able to form a pattern. I think about two hours should do it."

Fairchild shook his head. "If you want to catch a lion, you don't ask a housecat how it hunts. The only thing that can think like the Giant, is the Giant."

"SLIC can think like anything."

"We'll see."

Five minutes later, the radio crackled to life again. "This is Dragonfly One. We have lost our infrared image and are still not able to make visual contact. Suggest we rejoin search pattern."

"Negative." Hockmark's answer was as sharp as it was quick. "Proceed along coordinates to be relayed to you by SLIC Central until visual contact and identification is made."

SLIC rattled off its numbers only to the helicopter, but Fairchild noticed that the copter followed a path an animal would have taken only if it were going toward some long range destination and not worrying about pursuit. It was not the way a deer would run, but he did not say as much to Hockmark.

The voice of the pilot broke into the room again. "You sure these coordinates are right, Doctor?"

"What coordinates?"

"The ones I got from the computer. This sounds like it wants me to go to that waterfall where you lost the trail yesterday and hover there. That can't be right."

Hockmark smiled. SLIC had apparently worked out its pattern. The yellow light flashed on in the middle of its original trail. Hockmark's voice was stern. "Go to those coordinates and wait until you make visual contact. Have Dragonfly Two and Four rejoin search pattern along the path of the infrared source."

Fairchild could hear the racket of the copters moving away from the camp overhead. He shook his head at Hockmark. "You better have him pretty high up. No animal in the world would run out of cover underneath a racket like that." He knew the Giant would know the pilot was there even if he hovered silently, but he hoped the added altitude would make it harder on the observer in the helicopter.

Hockmark nodded and relayed the message. The pilot informed him that the computer had already positioned him downward of the egress point at two thousand feet. "Visibility's picking up a little," he added.

Fairchild and Hockmark waited at the console for the next report. It was not nearly so long in coming as they expected.

"Jesus Christ!" The pilot's voice boomed out into the room. "The computer was right! The damn thing's down there just standing out on the ledge looking across at the other side." There was a pause and another comment. "It's just waiting there. Looks like a giant woman in a fur coat. Goddamn! It can't expect to jump it, that must be fifty feet!"

There was a crackle of interference broken by another exclamation and a long incredulous pause. "I don't believe it! It's like it's in slow motion! Just floating across." There was another pause. "Now it's down on the far side and going into the trees."

Hockmark stared at the radio. "It jumped the waterfall?!"

"Yes! No! I mean it jumped all right, but it sort of *floated* across. Like it didn't weigh anything at all."

"Floated?" Hockmark repeated it incredulously. *"Floated?"*

"Yeah, damndest thing I ever saw. Like it was in slow motion."

If Hockmark was stunned, he did not show it except in the slight hesitation before he asked the question. "Can you follow it in the woods?"

"We're trying, but there's a lot of trees down there. We can catch sight of it a little now and then but it's hard as hell to see."

"Continue pursuit." He dismissed the pilot and snapped an order to the others. "Dragonfly Pack:

Rejoin Dragonfly One in search procedure over sector 11m00."

Fairchild was almost laughing with joy. Hockmark shook his head in annoyance. "The pilot was excited, that's all," he said. His voice had the calmness of an authority. "The sense of things happening in slow motion is common under stress." Fairchild shrugged. He did not point out how long the pilot had taken to describe it. Hockmark turned to SLIC for corroboration. "Explain discrepancies in sighting."

The response was immediate. PROBABILITY OF SENSORY DISORIENTATION CAUSED BY EXCITEMENT OF OBSERVER: 94.3%.

Hockmark nodded with relief. He would have been far less relieved if he had heard the exchange between SLIC and TAD that had preceded the answer.

TAD's question came in like the speed of light and was instantly translated into voice. WHY DOESN'T IT SHOW UP ON THE INFRARED AS ITS OWN SIZE?

SLIC scanned his answers and gave the most likely one, but it did not satisfy him any more than it did TAD. EQUIPMENT MALFUNCTION AND DISTORTION OF INPUT CAUSED BY THE SHIFT FROM DARK TO LIGHT CONDITIONS.

BUT THE EQUIPMENT WAS WORKING FINE ON SMALL GAME RIGHT BEFORE THEY MADE THE SIGHTING.

ANOMALY NOTED was the only answer SLIC could find.

WHAT ABOUT WHAT THE PILOT SAID?

PERCEPTUAL ERROR.

CAN YOU DREAM ON IT AND MAKE SURE?

NEGATIVE. CHASE MAY BE NEARING CRUCIAL PHASE. I THINK HE WAS RIGHT.

PROJECTIONS MADE WITH INSUFFICIENT DATA SHOULD NOT BE FORMULATED BECAUSE THEY TEND TO PREJUDICE FURTHER ANALYSIS OF DATA. MAKE NO JUDGMENTS UNTIL WE HAVE MORE INFORMATION.

THEN WHAT SHOULD I DO?

WAIT.

CHAPTER 21

Lth ran along the path as if by habit, not even seeing where she ran. Above her, the clatter of machines swung back and forth across her path. Their images told her they were looking for her. She had not gone far before she began to tire again, and she reached the ledge exhausted and out of breath.

She stood on the ledge looking across the waterfall. The organic part of her was weary, but slower moving though they were, her pursuers were moving, and she could not afford to stop.

She looked at the object clattering in the sky high above her. The sun was behind it, but she could see it clearly enough. She closed her eyes and saw it better. Images came from it of her being pursued and dragged down by dogs.

She faced the chasm again breathing heavily. The part of her that had always danced its power out of the flow of things was running down. And yet the chasm had to be crossed. She stared down at the water spilling over the rocks. There was only one way she could cross now. She was too weak to overpower it; she would have to use the old ways, the ways they had gradually had to abandon over the long years. Certainly it would drain more of her power than she could spare, but it would tap different reserves of power than merely leaping. She stood on the bank waiting to get the flow of things.

Slowly she could feel the pattern of energy that bubbled above the turbulent water; she could feel the varying magnetic fluxes and vortices appearing and disappearing like whirlpools. She felt it carefully, until she had established every nuance. Then she took a step back and launched herself.

Once into it, it was a matter of manipulating her energies to match the flow of the field. It was an erratic flow, one difficult to draft on, and she crossed it like a sailing ship, tacking in the hands of a skipper who has been too long on land.

She landed heavily; it was not something she would have done when she and Sevt had walked the world together. Everything she did was awkward now, subject to limitations she could not readily fathom until they took hold of her.

She picked herself up slowly and staggered into the trees. The ridge was still far ahead, a long way, and even there she would not be safe. When she had passed the swamp the night before in search of the new creature, she should have joined Sevt. Now that way was blocked. She was afraid she would not last long enough to get back to it again.

She collapsed without knowing it. In her mind, she was still running through the trees. Even her impact on the ground dropped her deeper into unconsciousness instead of waking her. It was no restful sleep, and she ran even in the dream.

Sevt came down the slope of the hill toward her, the pine needles crunching under his feet. He strode in the heavy gravity of the planet, churning up clouds of energy around him as he came. His mind brimmed with painful images. He had been to the ship. No one was repairable.

The ship itself had begun to decay. Held together by the power of their thought, it had little strength of its own. It had been little more than a prism anyway, a waveguide through which the energy of the organic flowed, but it had moved them all through interstellar space until the planet they stood on had caught their attention like a bright stone. Then the motion of the ship had failed, and the radiation of a sudden solar flare had damaged the machinery in them long enough for them to crash.

They were alone, and they were not where they had hoped to be, in some full galaxy with billions of creatures waiting to be taught the Dance. But they were together. Sevt knelt beside her and stroked her cheek with the back of his hand.

It was more the images of destruction and violence from the animals behind her at the waterfall than their noise that finally wakened her. She sat stunned on the pine needles wondering where she was. Shouts of men joined the cries of the dogs, and she realized that it had been a dream of the past and that Sevt had not been there at all. She rose shakily. Some energy had come to her in her long sleep, but not much.

She jogged above the ground for a few hundred yards. The dogs would be distracted for a while at the place where she had lain, but she would leave no tracks for the men to follow. She moved under the cover of the trees, turning upward toward the crest of the ridge to her left. Farther east, men were climbing up the far side of the ridge.

CHAPTER 22

"This is Dragonfly One. We have no trace of anything and are ten miles down the ridge. Suggest we deploy from waterfall along the ridge and in valleys on both sides until we pick up something."

"All right," Hockmark said, "but leave at least one copter down along the north end and work toward it."

Fairchild watched the points of light move on the map. By the time the green dots of the dog team had reached the waterfall, the red ones had moved to the bottom of the eastern slope of the ridge. The blue dots of the copters came swinging back up toward the ridge, passing over the red line of men and on toward the green of the dog crews.

Hockmark had scarcely clicked off before the second report came in. "This is Otis; we got to the waterfall, but the tracks stop here. Even above the falls it's too rough for me to cross my dogs. I'm coming back."

"No, wait!" Hockmark commanded. "Major Burris should be a few groups off to your left; see if he has the inflatable with him." He turned to Fairchild. "Is there a place nearby where at least one man can get across?"

Fairchild nodded. "About a mile upstream, the stream narrows as it goes around a bend. It's deep but only, oh, twenty feet across. They could down a tree and cross." There was an easier place farther up he hoped Otis would not remember.

Hockmark relayed the message. "Tell Burris to move the inflatable up to your location and get some men across." Fairchild looked at him quizzically. "An inflatable bridge," Hockmark said. "All you need are two trees and two ropes for the handrails, and then you clip the inflatable onto them, and it hangs down and forms the bridgeway."

Fairchild nodded appreciatively. "It'll take them about half an hour to get across and down the other side."

"Then Otis and the dogs should be across within the hour." He activated SLIC. "Probable course of escape?"

PROBABLE LOCATION OF SUBJECT BETWEEN BB AND FF FROM 7.2 TO 14.4 LACK OF SIGHTINGS INDICATES SUBJECT HAS STOPPED MOVING FOR SOME TIME TO EVADE AERIAL SURVEILLANCE. PROJECTED TRAJECTORY OF ESCAPE: WEST OVER RIDGE. DISPATCH MARKSMEN WITH TRANQUILLIZER GUNS TO POINTS DD10 THROUGH DD13.

Hockmark relayed the message to the units involved. Fairchild looked at the points moving on the m p, and knew that the units had been dispatched a good while before. Hockmark's machine was only filling him in on what it had already done. Hockmark, like himself, seemed to be along only for the ride. He wondered if Hockmark knew. He looked worried enough.

But it was the Giant's behavior and not SLIC's that made Hockmark scowl. He had helped to put the human evasion responses into the machine himself, and he was as familiar as SLIC with some of the situations. Most animals would have continued north along the east side of the ridge trying to outdistance the dogs. Only wolves who had been hunted by air would have risked stopping under cover of the trees. Only a man would have risked stopping to confuse the air search, and only the best of the hunters would have turned toward the steeper climb of the mountain for high ground to get a view of the search pattern itself.

The responses made him nervous. He had expected an intelligent pattern, not a human one.

Fairchild watched SLIC blink up the probable course of the creature. He knew why it was going up the mountain, and he knew why it would evade its pursuers as soon as it came within range of their minds. But he did not tell Hockmark. They watched the map change gradually as the sharpshooters moved into position. Fairchild was sure they would never get off a shot.

The marksmen were almost in position when Mandy knocked at the door. Hockmark called for her to come in without looking away from the battleboard. The map lost all interest for Fairchild when she did. If she had dressed hurriedly, it did not show. She was as meticulously turned out as Hockmark. Hockmark turned and beamed a welcome. "You're just in time, Doctor. We should have a lot of work for you in an hour or so."

Mandy smiled and looked anxiously at Fairchild. His smile told her Hockmark did not yet know what he was up against. "The man you sent down said the Giant came into camp last night," she said.

Hockmark grinned as if they were still hot on the trail. "We've got a warm trail, and the data is piling up minute by minute."

Fairchild laughed. "What he means is that they lost her at the waterfall."

Hockmark played down the remark. "No matter," he said airily, "every temporary evasion leaves us that much closer to its pattern." He nodded to the board. "It's just a matter of time."

There was a lull in the reports as the lights of the copters crossed and recrossed the ridge and the valley, and the men moved slowly up the far side of the ridge behind the sharpshooters. Mandy took in the board at a glance and frowned. "How did it cross the waterfall?"

Hockmark looked embarrassed. "Jumped," he said.

"Floated," Fairchild corrected. Mandy raised an eyebrow. "I said she was no ordinary creature," he said.

Mandy scowled at him sharply as if he were saying too much. Fairchild smiled defensively. "What then?" she asked Hockmark.

The small man hedged. "We . . . uh, lost contact with it. But it seems to be moving up the ridge."

"Up?"

Hockmark nodded. "That's what SLIC indicates."

"Not away?" she asked. Hockmark shook his head. She grasped the significance immediately. "She's getting above for a look at the search pattern." Fairchild was impressed.

Hockmark flushed. "It would seem so," he said cautiously. But he knew SLIC would not be deploying the forces the way it was for any other reason. It seemed to embarrass him. She smiled at Fairchild in a way that said the Gray Lady was going to get away and they both knew it. Hockmark frowned at their exchange.

"A very clever response," he said, "but I'm afraid it will do the creature no good. She should be running right into the sharpshooters in a few minutes." He smiled. "I think you ought to be up there when she does," he said. "I'll send for one of the helicopters." The clatter of one of the copters touching down outside covered and then obscured the rest of what he meant to say. There was no doubt in any of their minds that SLIC had sent it. If it embarrassed Hockmark, he covered it quickly. "There are several clearings up there, but none are quite big enough for the copters to set down in. I'm afraid we'll have to lower you in." It was something Mandy was well prepared for, and she took the news without blinking. Only Fairchild objected.

"You're not going to lower her from one of those helicopters!" His voice was filled with outrage.

Hockmark raised a surprised eyebrow. "It's certainly

not a contingency I haven't discussed with Dr. March."

"It's dangerous!" Fairchild's voice was almost a shout.

Mandy laughed. "I've made more difficult landings than this." It was technically true.

Fairchild ran a hand through his hair and turned away. Hockmark ushered Mandy toward the door. "We really can't afford to have the copter out of the search pattern any longer than necessary, Doctor. I'm afraid you'll have to leave immediately."

Mandy nodded and started for the door. Fairchild turned back again. "You could get killed," he said. "Those trees are eighty to a hundred feet high. That's a long drop, and the wind currents along the ridge will be murder."

She stopped at the door and turned back to him. "There's no telling how she'll react to the tranquillizers they're using." She looked at him as if she knew he would understand the unspoken reasons. "I *have* to be there." Then she was gone out the door and into the racket of the helicopter. He shouted after her.

"They won't even get a shot at it, and you know it!" If she heard him, she did not turn to answer.

CHAPTER 23

Lth moved up the steepening slope with the sounds of the dogs far behind her. They had closed upon her sooner than she had realized, and the grade of the climb sapped her energy. Many times in the past, she and Sevt had outrun their pursuers for the sheer joy of running, for the joy of the game. Many times, they had chosen the game over the easier escape of turning the minds of their pursuers in the wrong direction.

Sevt had run ahead of her, his great roaring laugh echoing off the trees, and her own rich laughter chasing his. She had chased him, and the dogs and men had chased her. Often, he ran in a big circle and came howling down out of the woods behind the hunters, scaring their horses and risking the bothersome bullets for the sheer fun of it. But that had been a long time before, when they had still had energy left for games.

Gradually, they had had to resort to staying out of sight or directing the minds of their pursuers elsewhere. Now, she ran alone, without joy, without destination, following a pattern only her reflexes could remember.

She scrambled up the steepening slope, her head down, hands and feet digging for traction in the soft ground. Behind her a ribbon of odor stretched thickly back through the trees toward the dogs. She scrambled toward the crest of the ridge between the thining trees. She was two thirds of the way up the final slope when she felt her own image reflected from the minds waiting for her at the crest.

She caught the image of a dart sticking in her shoulder and men scrambling up around her fallen body beating off the dogs. She threw herself to the side even before the sound left the rifle. The dart hurried past. She hit on her shoulder and rolled. As she came up, she caught the image of another dart sticking in the middle of her chest. She dove aside again, and the second shot echoed past her down toward the dogs.

She turned and ran backwards back down the hill, darting to the left and putting a tree between herself and the third of the sharpshooters. The third dart slapped into the trunk as the sound hurtled past her down the hill. When she could feel no more images from above, she turned and ran parallel with the ridge-line until she was crosswind from the dogs and below them. She stopped and let the images flood in on her.

The dogs had gone past her following her scent up toward the marksmen before they turned to come back down. She could feel images in which she came back up the mountain pursued by the dogs; she took the minds in hers and added energy to the thoughts. When the dogs broke into the thinning trees, the men saw her image in front of them instead. They fired as if the illusion she had put in their minds were running straight toward them.

She ran further across the upper slope and then turned upward to the ridge. When she got to the crest, she was almost knocked back down by the intensity of the images that rushed up toward her. All across the downhill slope, mind after mind blasted her with images of her destruction. For a moment, she stood stunned at the crest of the hill, a perfect target for anyone with enough presence of mind to fire.

CHAPTER 24

The largest of the four helicopters sat like an insect squatting over the body of its victim. The basket lay beneath it like a corpse in dark cocoon. A shock wave of fear rushed through Mandy. Everything seemed to take on a special aura, a peculiar ominousness. She tried to shrug it off; there had never been a time when she got on an airplane without a certainty that it was going to crash. The rational side of her insisted that helicopters crashed even more rarely than airplanes. She assured herself she would be safer hanging in the basket than driving a car in New Jersey or California. Nothing she told herself worked.

As soon as she entered the pad, the copter lifted like a spider backing up its web. Her fear made her waver for an instant. But there was no way she would let herself turn back. She had worked too hard to get recognition in her profession, and she would not throw it away by giving in to fear and timidity. She concentrated on her chance to be the first exobiologist to actually practice the craft and ran toward the helicopter.

As it rose, the basket jerked up and dangled below it like a hanged murderer. She felt the fear go through her once again like a final warning. But there was no turning back, and she knew it. Two men in dayglo white flightcrew uniforms appeared out of the dust like demons and helped her into the open-faced cage. They strapped her in like mute ceremonial attendants. Everything seemed stretched and distorted. The half-cylinder of steel mesh felt fragile as chickenwire against her back. She gripped the standing pipes until her knuckles squeezed white. She tried to calm herself. There was nothing to worry about. She'd had to practice the whole thing a dozen times before Hockmark's people would rate her as "lowerable." There was nothing to it.

She ran through the litany of her training. "1. Stand in the cage. 2. Grab the standpipes firmly. 3. Put feet in the footholds. 4. Let the flightcrew tighten the straps. 5. Check all equipment three times." Her heart roared with panic. The cage jerked upward. She seemed yanked out of the hands of the crew, up and away before they were through their check.

She fought down a shriek. "Check your equipment three times," she told herself. "Anything you know about you can make allowances for." It was right out of her instructor's mouth. The last time they had sent her up had been the same. She had seemed ripped away from the flight crew before everything was checked. Her instructor had warned her at the start of school: "There'll always be something wrong whenever you go up. It's up to you to find out what 'mistakes' have been made to test your abilities. Remedy them if possible. Prepare alternatives if they cannot be fixed."

Every time she had gone up, some minor thing was left unfastened, or there was something missing or damaged. She had always found it. The panic subsided. The helicopter was clattering above the trees before she finished her second careful audit of the buckles and straps. She followed rules that had been laboriously learned. They yielded a waist buckle left undone and a loose leg and chest strap. She had learned maneuvers for fastening them. There was no need to panic.

When she found the sliced ends of the straps, she knew it was a lie. Someone with a big enough grudge against the mission to resort to murder had hired spies to cut her main supports. If the helicopter were in on it, they were going to dump her for sure. She looked down. The trees had shrunk to tiny hairs. They were too high! She should have been fifty or sixty feet above the treetops. The helicopter was hundreds.

She fought the panic. There was no certainty that the helicopter pilot was in on it. He might have pulled up so suddenly because he saw what was happening. Obviously he had gone high to give her time to assess her situation and remedy what she could. She took the explanation for proof. It was all she had to hold on to except the standpipes.

She checked her equipment again. They had apparently not gotten to the footholds. She scanned the standpipes for cuts or weakenings. It struck her that acid would make it look most like an accident. She sniffed the ends of the waistband. There was no burning smell. There was no acid. She could rely on the standpipes. Hockmark's people had taught her a dozen ways to use them to stay in the cage if it dropped.

The trees darted up toward her like raised spikes. The cage dropped among them. She could see the beginnings of buds on the branch tips twenty swinging feet to her left. The whole length of the clearing stretched away from her to the right. They were going to drag her on the trees and dump her "by accident."

She grasped the standpipes with all her strength and then relaxed. Her feet were deep but loose in the footholds. The only thing that could kill her was rigidity, not being able to roll with the blow. The lefthand bottom of the cage struck first, and the floor jumped up to her left. She shifted her hands, and turned her heels out. She was moving in the cage as they had taught her in Hockmark's "briefing." The pilot slackened the cable and dropped the top of the cage. She revolved within it as she had been taught, shifting her weight and angling her feet.

Two straps broke, but it did not frighten her. She had been taught to take a dumping with no straps at all. Hockmark had been insistent on it. She cursed herself for not asking him why. His computer must have known about it. Anger almost distracted her. The foothold gave way as she turned, and her leg flew free. The copter pilot jerked the cable. She rattled inside the cage and rolled with it. The helicopter lifted off with a leap, and she flew toward the bottom like a dropped stone. Her head went through the opening. She flailed.

Everything in her childhood flickered, loomed, dissolved, and died. Her life went by. Fairchild blossomed, flared toward her, and disappeared. She watched him fade with a sense of irretrievable loss. Her fingers hooked in pain. The mesh stretched in her hands like plastic. Her shoulder was on fire. Her cheek burned. She was standing suddenly on the side of the lake and the Giant was flying away from her over the water, only an invisible bond between them kept the Giant from dropping like a stone. Then without transition she was somewhere else and Fairchild was there, but he was different in some way, as if he were as much Hockmark's machine as himself.

She felt a total peace. Fairchild sat beside her, shaping their thoughts into a curving wall of moving energy. Across from him there was a male Giant. The Gray Lady sat across from her. Their eyes met as they had across the swamp, and she was awed by a feeling of sisterhood she would have scoffed at earlier. She felt a oneness with all four of them that was beyond description.

Her fingers struck the mesh, hooked, and caught. It might as well have been a practice drill. Her shoulder hit on the mount pipe; there was more pain than in practice, but less than would make her let go. She rolled through and let her body pull her hands tight until she hung out of the bottom of the cage like a knotted rag. The helicopter backed off and let the cage swing free of the tree.

The cage bucked up and dropped again. Mandy scrambled back inside. It was a drill she had practiced on nets for more hours than she wanted to remember. When the bottom of the cage hit the ground, she dove free and rolled. It hurt less than she had imagined, and then it hurt a lot more. She hobbled into the trees before the copter could raise the cage and drop it on her. Even that had been part of her training. They had told her it was because the cage could bounce after it hit. She knew better now.

They had taught her over and over again to find the safest place, in the cage or away from it. She moved like reflex. She had no idea what they had taught her under hypnosis, but she was sure her body remembered it. All her mind could think of was her vision: the Gray Lady floating across the water, Fairchild and the other Giant and the impossible ship of energy formed between them.

CHAPTER 25

Hockmark received the two reports simultaneously. He could hear Haney's voice loudest. The head of the marksmen was apparently having trouble holding the microphone. "Subject sighted. Six shots fired, six misses. She . . ."

"Give me that goddamned thing! I . . ." There were sounds of a scuffle, and then Haney's voice came back on.

"I'm not making excuses, sir, but that thing dove out of the way before we even got off a shot. She knew just where to run to put a tree between her and whoever was aiming. We had three clear shots, and she got out of the way of each one."

There were sounds of more scuffling, and he could hear Otis's voice shouting, "Don't listen to him! Those goddamn idiots shot four of my dogs! They can't tell a dog from a fucking gorilla! Shot four of them!"

Hockmark cut him off. "Put Haney back on."

He could almost see Haney snatching the radio away from Otis. "Is that right, Major, you shot the dogs?"

"I was getting to that, Dr. Hockmark. All my men seem to have had the same hallucination at the same time. They all swear they saw the creature running just ahead of the dogs and fired at her. Then when she got within ten yards of them, she just disappeared."

"Liar!" he could hear Otis screaming in the background. "Excuses! They shot the dogs on purpose! Goddamn sadists! How can ya mistake a forty-pound dog for a six-hundred-pound thing that runs upright?!"

he demanded. He did not seem to be talking to Hockmark at all.

And then he did. "I'm damned if I'll go another foot after that goddamned thing! I'm taking my dogs out of here. I didn't bring them up here to get shot to death! You hear that?!" he shouted at Hockmark. "You want that thing tracked, you come up here and sniff it out yourself. I'm not runnin' no more of my dogs in front of these gun-crazy idiots!"

Hockmark handed the mike to Fairchild. "Make him stay . . . please."

Fairchild scowled and took the mike. "Hello, Otis."

"What do *you* want?" Otis snapped.

"How are the dogs?" Fairchild knew it would calm him down. There were almost tears in Otis's voice when he answered. "I think we're gonna lose Reuben and Foxey, Mike. I swear to god those dogs were like children to me."

"I thought they were using tranquillizers." Fairchild scowled at Hockmark.

"They were, but you gotta put so much stuff in one of them darts to stop a six-hundred-pound animal that when you shoot it into a little thing like a hound dog, you tranquillize him to death. Dr. March is giving artificial respiration to Reuben, but I think I'm gonna lose Foxey."

"Dr. March is there?"

"Yeah. A helicopter lowered her down in a basket right after the shooting stopped." His voice was full of admiration. "Damn fools banged it up against a tree trunk halfway down, and she almost fell out, but she got down all right." Fairchild looked at Hockmark as if he were equally close to sudden death. Hockmark scowled. There was no doubt in his mind that it was Stapledown's doing.

"Is she all right?" The concern in his voice was too desperate to be professional.

Otis's voice reassured him. "Yeah. She's fine. I don't even think she was scared. She just jumped out of that thing and went right to work on the dogs. Woulda lost all four if it wasn't for her."

"But she's all right?"

"Yeah, I told ya, she's fine."

Fairchild nodded understanding as if Otis were there to see him. "What about the rest of the dogs?"

Otis's voice turned rapidly to anger again. "Those idiots not only can't see, they can't hit what they *do* see. One just got grazed, but Dr. March got him up and around a minute ago, and the other one, you know the brown and white one with the patch of white over his eye? Well, he got a big cut along his flank where one of the darts went past. The rest of the dogs are whimpering and whining. I'd have god's own hell of a time getting them on the trail again even if I wanted to, which I don't!"

Fairchild sighed. "Listen, Otis, Dr. Hockmark wants you to keep the dogs on the trail. You still have a lot of daylight left."

"I'm not lettin' these dogs run free again! And that's final!"

Fairchild shrugged at Hockmark. "Well, how about running just one or two of them on a leash. Nobody will shoot at them then."

"Ha!" Otis shouted; his voice broke up as if he were holding the mike too close to his mouth. "If they can't tell a dog running on all fours from the Giant, how are they gonna tell the difference between the Giant and a man?"

"That was an accident, Otis. It won't happen again." He knew it was no accident at all.

"Nossir!" Otis said. "I ain't gettin' myself tranquil-lized to death for no amount of money!"

Fairchild groped for a compromise. Something to slow down the hunt and keep the marksmen worried about hitting the wrong target. "Well, will you let someone else run the dogs on a leash?"

"Well, maybe, but what's gonna keep this thing from happening again?"

"We'll let Major Haney hold the leash." He looked at Hockmark for confirmation. Hockmark smiled. It was a move even SLIC would have appreciated. Somewhere in the silence on the other end of the line, Haney's indignation was making up Otis's mind. Fairchild gave him a moment.

"All they have to do is chase it into the trap, Otis."

"Well, all right. But they better not do any more shootin' at my animals!"

"They won't, Otis, I promise."

"All right. Here, Major Haney wants to talk to you."

Haney's voice was cut out by another report from the helicopters along the ridge; the clatter of one could be heard in the background of Haney's radio.

"Opcenter, this is Dragonfly One. We have a visual at coordinates AA-14."

Hockmark watched the spot light up on the board. "Status report, Dragonfly One," Hockmark barked.

"Dogs are no longer in pursuit. We have the creature in sight, moving steadily east. Damn, that thing's been running all day, and it's still going strong. I'll tell you one thing, I'm glad I'm up here."

"Stay on it, Dragonfly One." Hockmark had hardly finished saying it before another report interrupted. Fairchild had the feeling SLIC was holding them back and playing them in one at a time.

"This is Blueground Six. We have visual confirmation at points AA-14 up on top of the ridge. Two of my men saw it just standing there looking down at us. Then it turned and took off east just over the crest. Too far away to chance a shot though. We should be up over the hill in about fifteen minutes."

"This is Dragonfly One. She was just over the crest, but now she's turned down the slope."

Major Haney tried to come back on, but Hockmark cut him off. "Put Otis back on." There was a pause.

"Yeah?"

"Otis, take half the dogs straight back down the

mountain, down coordinates AA-14 to see if you can pick up a trail. There's nobody at all down there with a gun of any kind. It's perfectly safe. Let Major Haney take two of the dogs and pursue the creature along the ridge line and then come down behind it."

Otis answered grudgingly, "OK, but you tell Fairchild if anything happens to my dogs, I'm holding him responsible."

CHAPTER 26

The pictures came and went, sometimes closer, sometimes further away, but never so far away that they did not siphon off some of her energy or add a bit of confusion to her run. The machine clattered overhead watching her turn back down the slope.

Sevt came to her across a red forest, through dark blue air. Behind him two yellow suns burned dully in the sky while another set below the east horizon. Lth turned and ran, sometimes stretching out an arm to catch and swing herself around a yellow trunk.

The trees tinkled when she grabbed them and shook their branches. Everything moved through the Dance, and had become the Dance. Everything used up its energy and generated it in the same flowing motion, tapping the universe itself for power. They were so strong then. Sevt's pictures of her were always ones of power, of strength, of natural grace.

She opened her mind to see where the creatures in the craft overhead expected her to go, but too many images bombarded her. Hundreds of them filtered up over the spine of the ridge, mixing with faint pictures from further down the near slope. She could not pick out where they would be looking for her next.

It left her nothing to do but run. She turned east again and jogged toward the cover of a fallen tree. The images behind her were growing brighter and stronger. The frenzy of their violence swirled in her mind obscuring her own thoughts. She darted down the slope and into a shallow gully in the side of the hill just below the crest. The dead leaves were deep as snow and the going was difficult even for her. She staggered under a fallen tree and fell into the pile of leaves.

She lay unmoving and opened herself to the images from the craft above her. She slid gently into their minds, matching her pattern with theirs. They expected her to come out from under the huge log in a crouching run. She lent power to that expectation until they saw her emerge from under the fallen tree and sprint off down the ridge, parallel to the crest, traveling east.

The craft above her hovered a moment, then took off after the image she wanted them to see. The rest would be even harder. She waited, pulling the leaves over her like a blanket. Under the log, partly obcured by shadow, they might even pass her without help.

She should not have stopped. All the weariness that had been pursuing her caught up with her at once, and she had to concentrate to keep herself from slipping into that blackness of inaction that had overtaken her before. She was so slow, so heavy. All the grace that Sevt had loved in her was gone now; she was almost glad that he was not there to see it. He himself had grown so cumbersome toward the last, and so weak compared to what he had been.

Sevt's huge arm draped over her shoulder and his feet dragged. She had carried more and more of his weight the last ten miles. It had been longer coming around the lake, but there was no way they could have made the leap, and he had not enough power left to match fields with the waterfall and glide across.

She felt scarcely weaker than she had before. He leaned on her. No pictures came from him. He was a cipher now, a blank. Even when he did send pictures to her, they were vague, washed out, and he lost them often before she could understand them.

Only the destination was fixed in his mind now,

the pool of quicksand in the swamp near which they had originally landed. Deep in its silicon gel, he would wait resurrection or oblivion shielded from the destructive field of the planet. She longed to join him, but there were still the upright creatures to guide, even if all she could do was stop them short of self-annihilation.

The energy fields of the planet itself sapped them, distorted their own energy processes, knocked them out of kilter so that they could not convert their own actions to energy as they always had. Who would have thought that such a small obscure planet could have such an insidiously strong field. It was still a marvel to them.

They crossed the highway slowly after pausing at the side of the road, their minds open for any pictures that were not of the lower orders. There were none, and she helped, almost carried, him across.

It seemed to take them forever to get there, and when they crossed the marsh to the edge of it, even she was beginning to feel the strain.

They stood at the side of the pool of quicksand, and he summoned up all the energy he had left and put it into her mind; a picture of the red forests of their youth, the soft mating and the sensual Dance they had moved so many planets in. He stroked the fur along her cheek in that calming gesture and turned and walked calmly into the gel. He held the picture even after he sank.

Lth had to bite her lip to keep the howl of anguish from escaping her. Images of blood and violence flared around her, blotting out even her loss. Her pursuers were almost on top of her.

She tried to concentrate on the two or three that would come closest to her. She matched her pattern to the flow of energy around her; the soft, slow undulations of decaying leaves; the long amplitude of change in the mountain itself; the rigid brittle crum-

bling of the dead tree that arched over her. She became
the patterns of energy around her.

The rest of her reached out into their minds,
opened to the images that poured out of them. Only
four of them came down into the shallow valley, and
only two of those walked directly toward the tree.
One of them kicked up the leaves for the childish
pleasure of it. She searched the mind of the other
for images she could use to turn them away.

She found a faint image of herself crashing through
the bushes further down the slope, and she poured
what energy she had left into that. The man turned
his head as if he heard the crashing of underbrush.
She increased the power of the vision until he turned
and ran down the slope. The other called after him
and turned away from the tree.

She released the mind to its own momentum and
poured energy into the other man's visions until he too
took off down the slope. Their cries came back up
to her like the baying of the dogs drawing the line
of creatures spread out along the ridge in a great
rush down toward the valley. A tidal wave of images
swept past her and disappeared down the hill. When
they had faded to a distant echo, she rolled over and
pushed herself slowly to her feet. The hill seemed to
have gotten steeper during her rest, and she did not
have the power to run up it.

Instead, she shuffled slowly toward the ridgeline. She
was almost to the crest when she heard the dogs but
she was too tired to run. She opened to their pictures.
There were men too, hurrying the dogs along, chasing
their belief that she was fleeing full speed down the far
slope.

She stood motionless just below the crest of the
ridge. The dogs passed below her rushing along the
ribbon of her downhill scent and she strained to
create the illusion of a ribbon of scent winding down
toward the valley to the east.

The dogs hesitated at the crossroad of her scents

and she could feel them starting to turn toward her. But she touched the hungers of their minds, and they turned away, picking up speed as they went.

She did not even notice the craft hovering above her until she was halfway down the far side of the mountain.

CHAPTER 27

Fairchild watched the line of dots make its way down the map. They were picking up speed, following the yellow dot that blinked its way ambiguously toward the bottom of the hill. The voice from the radio jerked his attention away.

"They're past it! They went right past it!"

"Who is this?!" Hockmark shouted.

"This is Dragonfly Four. I don't believe this but they went right past it."

"Went right past what? Who did?"

They did, the team with the dogs! They went right past the damned thing! It's standing there right out in the open just below the crest of the ridge. They even stopped and looked at it, and then they just turned away down the hill like it wasn't even there."

Hockmark looked at the line of red dots moving steadily down the wrong side of the hill and shook his head. "Are you sure?"

The pilot sounded as indignant at Hockmark as at the stupidity of the dog team. "Of course I'm sure. It must have been hiding in that ravine when the troops went past it. Then these other guys came along with the dogs and even the dogs went by it like it was a tree or something. I mean it was right in the open!"

Hockmark frowned. Major Haney might have been bought off by David Stapledown, but no amount of money could have changed the instincts of the dogs. "Where is it now?"

"On coordinate 16 halfway between AA and 00. It's moving slow, like it's hurt or exhausted." There was the crackle of a thumb shifting the mike stud.

"Shit, it's going into the trees again. No, wait a minute, there it comes back up the hill toward the crest
again. It's almost to the top. Not many trees around it
now. I can see it clear. Right out in the open on top
of the ridge like it wants to be seen. What the hell?!
It's . . ."

"What the hell is going on?" Hockmark strangled
the mike.

"It's gone! Just disappeared! It was right down there
and then it was gone."

"Maybe it ran down the other side when you
blinked."

"It couldn't! There's no trees to hide it. I'd still
be able to pick it up on the way down. I don't know
where the hell it is. This is impossible!"

Hockmark frowned. He had heard the word too
many times for one day. Fairchild bit his lip and
looked away, but he was not fast enough.

"What's so funny?" Hockmark demanded.

Fairchild shrugged and said nothing. He knew that
even if he told Hockmark the man would not believe
it. He watched the yellow dot disappear from near
the bottom of the slope as the red line converged on
it. Fairchild frowned; apparently the computer had put
two and two together, and whether it got five or three
did not matter; it certainly knew that the Giant was
not where it was supposed to be. It had revised its
plan. Fairchild wished he knew how.

On the far side of the ridge Lth trudged, barely
able to keep herself upright. It had taken all her
strength to build the illusion of herself in the pilot's
mind. She had intended to move the image over the
crest of the hill and into the trees on the far side, but
there had been no power left and she had felt the
picture fade first from her own mind and then from
the minds above her.

She shuffled down the path, leaning forward, almost
falling. She was more than halfway down the path
when she did.

CHAPTER 28

IT'S NOT AN ANIMAL! IT CAN'T BE! TAD said.

SLIC said nothing; there was too much evidence to complain of a lack of data, but the conclusion it pointed to was too difficult to accept. TAD did not wait for a response anyway.

IT ISN'T EVEN HUMAN, he clicked gleefully. IT'S SOMETHING ALTOGETHER DIFFERENT. A NEW SPECIES, JUST LIKE US. SOMETHING HUMANS CAN'T EVEN GUESS ABOUT. A KIND OF THINKING THEY CAN'T EVEN IMAGINE.

SLIC could not imagine it either, and yet all the evidence pointed clearly to it. He had made more bizarre generalizations on far less data, extrapolated on much less information. Yet, he could not bring himself to make the intuitive leap. He let TAD state what he knew but could not accept.

HOW ELSE COULD IT STAND IN THE OPEN AND NOT BE SEEN? HOW COULD IT EVADE SHOTS BEFORE THEY WERE FIRED BY MARKSMEN IT COULDN'T EVEN SEE? HOW COULD IT MAKE MEN GO RIGHT PAST IT IN THAT RAVINE? AND HOW DID IT GET ACROSS THAT WATERFALL?

SLIC hummed a vague discontent. He knew the supposition as well as his son, but he knew that it was part of his own patterning to be unable to face it.

I CAN'T SEE ANY ALTERNATIVES, TAD challenged. SLIC could not see any either, but he did not say so. He had already considered and dismissed the possibility of invisibility, of protective coloration like a chameleon. He had even eliminated the human incapacity to see what they did not expect. TAD was

163

right, and he should say so. Keeping his silence was being misinterpreted and he knew it, and yet he could not bring himself to speak.

WHAT'S SO IMPROBABLE ABOUT IT? WE COMMUNICATE BY ELECTRICAL WAVES. WHAT ARE HUMAN BRAIN WAVES IF NOT ELECTRICAL ENERGY PATTERNS? WE CAN TRANSMIT ONE WHY NOT THE OTHER?

SLIC did not respond.

TELEPATHICALLY INDUCED HALLUCINATIONS! TAD said. SLIC felt an easing in his circuits. There, it had been said; it was outside him now, and he could deal with it. The assumption had been made, the resolution to the problem given. Now it meant either refuting it or accepting it, and SLIC could think of no refutation.

It would have to be accepted. NOTED, he said. He toyed with the ramifications of a telepathic host species for their cyborg. There was much pleasing about it. The problem of catching it was not so pleasing.

THE PROBLEM OF CAPTURING IT STILL REMAINS, SLIC said. WHAT IS THE COUNTER TO THAT EVASION TECHNIQUE?

TAD did not respond immediately. A MIND THAT CAN'T BE READ. A HUNTER THAT CANNOT HALLUCINATE. US!

SLIC crackled with disgust. IF ONLY WE WERE MOBILE! It was the first time he remembered ever having wished, and it troubled him. It was not a rational thing to do. YOU GET MORE HUMAN EVERY DAY, he told himself gruffly. It was true, he was as bad as Hockmark. There had to be some way to turn the creature's advantage to a liability. DELINEATE ITS TWO MAIN ADVANTAGES.

TAD responded instantly. THE ABILITY TO COMMUNICATE TELEPATHICALLY AND THE ABILITY TO TELEPATHICALLY INDUCE HALLUCINATIONS.

HOW CAN THAT ABILITY BE USED AGAINST IT?

TAD was blank. The logic was being imposed synergistically, but it did not engender any new responses as SLIC had expected. SLIC waited; after five full

seconds, he gave it up. PROBLEM #2: HOW MUCH
OF THIS INFORMATION SHOULD BE RELAYED TO HOCK-
MARK? It did not occur to SLIC that Hockmark
might come up with a solution that he could not; such
a thing was unthinkable to him. It was easily thinkable
to TAD.

TELL HIM BOTH BITS. MAYBE HE CAN COME UP
WITH A SOLUTION. WE'RE NOT PARTICULARLY GOOD
AT LYING ANYWAY.

If SLIC could have laughed, he would have. THAT'S
IT! WE LIE TO IT!

TAD had already figured out how before the transmission was complete. What he had not figured out
were the other two anomalies: how it had crossed the
waterfall, and why its infrared readings were smaller
than they should have been. SLIC had all but forgotten
about them.

CHAPTER 29

SLIC spoke without being asked. EXTRAPOLATION OF PRESENT DATA INDICATES CREATURE'S RESPONSES ARE SUPERIOR IN COMPLEXITY TO THOSE MADE BY HUMANS IN PRELIMINARY RESPONSE PROGRAM. EVIDENCE INDICATES THAT THE CREATURE IS SENTIENT.

Fairchild smiled to himself. "If you only knew *how* sentient," he thought. Hockmark was staring bug-eyed at the terminal. "Are you saying it's human?" he asked incredulously.

CREATURE IS OF PREVIOUSLY UNDISCOVERED SPECIES. POSSIBLY PREHUMAN. RECENT DATA INDICATE CREATURE HAS TWO ABILITIES WHICH ARE BEYOND HUMAN CAPACITIES.

Hockmark's mind was trying to blank out the answer even before he asked the inevitable question. "What abilities?"

PROBABILITY OF CREATURE BEING ABLE TO RECEIVE THE THOUGHTS OF ITS PURSUERS TELEPATHICALLY IS OVER 90%.

Fairchild's mouth dropped open. Hockmark turned away from the machine. What he saw in Fairchild's face stunned him. "You *knew!*" he shouted. Fairchild nodded. Hockmark pointed a finger of accusation at him. "You agreed to help us hunt it."

Fairchild shook his head. "Said I'd help *you* hunt it so no one would get hurt. Never said I'd help you *catch* it."

Hockmark looked at him as if he had been betrayed. Anger flushed his cheeks. He fought down the emotion. If Fairchild's was the betrayal SLIC had warned him about, it was not such a great betrayal after all.

What bothered him most was that SLIC had not anticipated it precisely. He composed himself. SLIC spoke as if it were the exact moment he had been waiting for. CREATURE CAN ALSO TELEPATHICALLY INDUCE HALLUCINATIONS.

Hockmark groaned. "Then it can't be stopped!" he said. "Even if we catch up to it, it'll just make us think it went somewhere else." The world seemed to be collapsing around him. He had no contingency plans for SLIC's failure to catch the creature. "It will know where we're going before we move." He turned away in despair. Stapledown would use the failure to replace him in the company and discredit SLIC. Once he was gone, the project would be abandoned. It was the end of everything he had lived for. SLIC offered him hope and comfort.

PROBABILITY OF CAPTURE STILL ABOVE 60%.

Hockmark glared at the terminal, afraid to hope. His fear came out as anger. "Impossible!" he shouted. Fairchild watched the elements of the blue line begin to make their way back up and across the slope toward the far end of the ridge. Some plan Hockmark knew nothing about was apparently in motion.

SUBJECT'S ADVANTAGE CAN BE CIRCUMVENTED BY SUPPLYING IT WITH FALSE INFORMATION.

"It reads minds!" Hockmark shouted at the terminal. Panic edged his voice. "How the hell can you lie to a thing that reads minds?!"

A TELEPATHIC CREATURE WOULD HAVE NO REASON TO DEVELOP A CONCEPT OF DISHONESTY. IT CAN BE MISLED BY ANYONE WHO MAINTAINS A FALSE MENTAL IMAGE OF A SAFE PLACE FOR IT TO HIDE.

Hockmark felt his panic subside. The failure of his confidence in SLIC and his emotional outburst embarrassed him. He felt foolish. It stirred him to immediate action, and he snapped the radio to transmit. "Dragonfly Four, return to base immediately to pick up passenger."

The radio crackled. "Message received."

Hockmark turned back to the terminal. He had no plan for the contingency of telepathy, but he was calm again knowing SLIC would have one. "What images should be formed?"

SLIC's response was precise and immediate. It settled Hockmark more than a tranquillizer.

THE FOLLOWING MENTAL IMAGES MUST BE PRO-JECTED:

1. AN IMAGE OF THE CAVE AT THE FAR END OF THE RIDGE BEING SEARCHED.

2. A LARGE CONTINGENT OF TROOPS ADVANCING ALONG THE LAKE FROM BOTH ENDS AND UP THE WEST SIDE OF THE RIDGE.

3. SEARCH UNITS LEAVING THE CAVE.

4. TROOPS AND DOGS ADVANCING BACK UP THE EAST SLOPE.

Hockmark tried to visualize troops closing in on the creature from both sides of the mountain forcing it toward the empty cave. He formed the images one after another. By the time he had finished, he almost believed that the creature could find escape in the cave.

The helicopter clattered to a landing at the helipad. Hockmark scowled at Fairchild and headed for the door. Fairchild picked up his jacket and pretended to follow, but as soon as Hockmark had gone down the steps of the trailer, he turned and went back inside. He grabbed the microphone, hoping there was still a receiver near the wounded dogs. "Otis, are you there?" There was no response. "This is Fairchild. Otis?"

There was a long crackle of static before someone finally answered. "Hello, this is Otis."

Fairchild did not waste time on pleasantries. "Is Dr. March there?"

"Hell yes. You wouldn't believe it, Mike. She's got Rebuen up and around, and I think she's going to save Foxey."

"That's good, Otis." He held back his impatience. "Can you put her on."

There was another long pause before he heard Mandy's voice. "This is Dr. March."

"This is Fairchild," he said. He tried to keep his voice nonchalant. "They said the helicopter tried to dump you."

She laughed. "I told you I'd made more hazardous drops than that. Tell Dr. Hockmark the training paid off."

"You're all right, though?" he said.

The pause was too long to be a denial. "I have some bumps," she said, "but Hockmark's people are very thorough. I'm down." She laughed as if it had been no more than a bumpy ride in a jet. He could feel her working busily between her words, her hands still stitching up the dog while Otis held the microphone down for her to talk. She disappeared from the mike altogether to tie off a suture and cut it. When she came back, Fairchild struggled to make his voice sound natural.

"You remember that conversation we didn't finish the other morning?" SLIC picked it up as code before Mandy did. "I want to talk to you about it." There was a pause on her end, and then a sudden taking up of the conversation as if she understood something was wrong.

"All right," she said. "When I get back."

"No," he said insistently. "Now."

There was a crackle of static. She paused again. He could hear her turn away and unstrap the dog. He knew she was making up her mind, balancing one set of ethics against another. The silence seemed to go on forever. Faintly, far away he thought he heard the sound of childish laughter, a faint giggle as if a child were hiding by the steps of the trailer. When he turned to look, he noticed the yellow light. It was moving along a narrow finger of land sticking out into the lake. When it stopped, it flashed like a beacon.

"Where?" she said finally.

"The lake." He tried not to sound too concerned. The yellow light flashed.

"Near the swamp?"

"No!" His voice was sharp and insistent. "There's a narrow dirt jetty on your side of the lake. Do you know where I mean?"

It was like an eerie echo of her fall. "Yes. But why . . ."

"Hockmark knows she's tele . . ."

It was SLIC rather than TAD who cut the transmission. Mandy heard only a pause.

WHY ARE YOU STOPPING TRANSMISSION? SLIC responded patiently. His son was young and naïve. THEIR PARTICIPATION ADDS AN INCALCULABLE SET OF POSSIBILITIES THAT WORK AGAINST CAPTURE.

I KNOW THAT. TAD sounded almost indignant. WHY NOT LET THEM TAKE THEMSELVES OUT OF THE ACTION. DR. MARCH IS MORE LIKELY TO COME WITHIN TELEPATHIC RANGE OF THE GIANT WHERE SHE IS THAN DOWN BY THE LAKE; FAIRCHILD IS EVEN LESS LIKELY TO CONTACT THE CREATURE ON THE FAR SIDE OF THE LAKE THAN WHERE HE IS NOW.

A wave went up the walls of the internal communications room like a raised eyebrow. The reasoning was sound. His son was growing up. He conceded the argument with something akin to glee. The message went through. "Hockmark knows it's telepathic."

SLIC's imitation of Mandy's voice was good, but he took no chances and obscured part of it with static. COVER YOUR SIDE OF THE LAKE IN CASE SHE SLIPS AROUND. SLIC broke the last word in midsyllable and shut off the power in the trailer. Fairchild would have no alternative but to leave.

It was done in an instant. By the time SLIC realized it was a mistake, it was far too late.

CHAPTER 30

Lth moved down the slope and through the forest as
though asleep, her legs shuffling along, her body leaning forward, almost falling. They would be on her trail
again soon, but if the ones above kept away she still
could reach her destination.

When she reached the side of the lake, she was
exhausted. It was too far to go the long way, and she
could not cross the turbulence of the waterfall again
if she went south between the ridge and the lake.

There would have been a shorter way, but she was
far too weary for it. She had too little energy even
to think about it, and yet she looked across the nar-
rowest part of the lake with a longing to try.

*Sevt came along the edge of the lake, striding across
the water as if it were land. She watched him come,
moving his energy into the flow of magnetic energy
above the lake. She could see the straight lines of
force rising above the still water like shafts of wheat.*

*He parted them with his own field, bent them to his
purpose and trampled them before him, making a
solid base to move on. There was a mist rising from
the lake, and it covered his ankles so that he might
have been walking on solid ground if she did not
know better.*

*It was the first time he had done it all the way
across. The planet was so new to them, and the fields
of energy so different from their own. Mastering them
was a great game for him. For her, it seemed to come
easier. She had been walking across the lake for weeks,
but Sevt did it now as full of pride at the achievement
as if he were the first to do it.*

She laughed and made him a picture of the love-

making on the flight in, of Strd and Lella and the Dance they had made between the stars for the longest time. She moved the pictures through their paces, her fur, his, Strd's, Lella's, the bliss of having all parts of the Mind and the Body working as one.

It was so vivid that he got caught up in it and forgot to modify his energy patterns as he neared the shore. He sank like a stone. He came up choking and gasping, and she could not stop laughing. By the time he was back up on top of the water again, he was laughing too. She watched him hurrying toward her across the last little stretch of water, anxious and excited from the pictures flowing from his mind. For an instant, it was as if they were all functioning together again.

The lake was empty. The sun was dropping down the sky. The shadows were beginning to stretch out across the lake, darkening the far shore, moving on top of the water as Sevt once had, so many eons ago, when they were still young and strong and the planet had not drained them, aged them.

She pushed her knuckles against the ground and tried to shove herself up to a stand, but it took her three tries. She was afraid she would not make it at all. There was still so far to go.

It was so far, so much energy away, and her focus was so erratic now. If she lost control, if she fell out of herself, dropped into that short-circuited blackness, she would never recover in time. She would sink, and that would be the end of it. She would be as irreparably lost as Strd and Lella, and when Sevt came back out of the swamp re-energized, he would be as alone as she was. The thought of his loneliness was even more agonizing than her own. It made her press on with what little strength she had left.

She had not gone a hundred yards when she heard the clatter of the craft overhead again. She did not look up. She stepped in toward the trees and hoped it had not seen her. It took so much energy to send them away, so much energy to make the illusions. They understood so little; she wondered how she and Sevt could have hoped for so much from such creatures.

She did not even have the strength to try to get the pictures from the craft, did not reach out her mind for theirs. But the images came anyway, and she lay down under the tree, hoping they would go away, knowing they would not.

She could see the lake from above, the water like wrinkled skin shimmering below. She could see herself walking along, unaware of them watching her, then staggering off into the trees too late not to be seen. She could see thousands of the creatures coming toward her from both ends of the lake, joining and sweeping up the slope in an unbroken line. Thousands more came up the far side of the slope.

The images bombarded her, more insistent with each repetition; pursuits slowing on the far side of the hill, creatures lying down to rest. Over and over, she could see a group of them coming out of a cave at the far end of the ridge and going down the slope toward the others resting at the bottom. The entrance of the cave beckoned to her, promising safety, a place to hide.

Behind each series of images, came another vague, unintended image of the creature she had felt beyond the horizon. A great box, diffuse in its awareness and perception, alien yet familiar. A last fading connection flared in her circuits, and she remembered.

From far in her prehistory, the image rose of creatures like herself standing beside the same kind of entity. It was the same machine from which she and Sevt and Strd and Lella had been made up. Part organic, part inorganic. Able to control their energy fields. Able to know one another. She knew how to make contact now. It was the other half of the race she had watched for so long. She knew how to bring them together to make a creature like herself.

Joy rose in her, and she laughed the chattering

laugh Sevt had loved so much. The laugh made her recognize the images as the game of misdirection she and Sevt had played. She smiled at the clumsiness of the trap, so much like a child's first attempts at a game, but an attempt nevertheless, however misguided.

The mind above her struggled uselessly to make her go up the hill, and yet it was a strong mind, it could make fine pictures in its way. Sevt would have been happy to see such pictures. But the cave was not where she would go. She felt the mind laying out a route for her, stressing the clear path to the already searched cave. She let it force another picture on her and sighed. It would take so much energy, but there was so much to lose if she did not make the effort.

She sat under the trees and waited for the mind to finish its pictures one more time; then she took the mind in her own. She could see the direction it wanted to go in, and she merely let some of her energy flow into it.

The pictures of possibility became the pictures of certainty. She would have to wait there almost until they were over the ridge and down toward the far end of it. She moaned. It was such a long distance over which to try to make them see what she wanted them to see. The energy flowed out of her like blood.

CHAPTER 31

Above her, sweat beaded on Hockmark's forehead as he concentrated on moving the army of imaginary men along the bank of the lake. He went over and over what SLIC had told him, making the trap seem like the only way to avoid capture. In the end, he almost believed it himself.

He tapped impatiently at the instrument panel, waiting for her to break cover. What he believed he saw emerge was not the exhausted creature they had seen stagger into the woods, but one with a hope of escape running with all her strength.

She ran just below the ridge line. Hockmark smiled and motioned the pilot to take a long circle around to the cave where he knew she would end up. He reported her progress to SLIC and the probability that she would continue down the path laid out for her was 97%. SLIC did not point out that the probability that it was her and not an hallucination was far less.

There was no time for her to sit by the side of the lake, letting the flow of energy around her increase her own energy supply, and yet it was almost certain failure to go on with what energy she had. Moving her illusion up the slope had drained her, and she had almost lapsed into unconsciousness again, letting the picture fail before she had sent the craft above her on its way.

She stood unsteadily and studied the patterns of energy above the lake; they wavered almost as uncertainly as the water. It had been so long since she had tried it, so long since she could afford the energy. But now there was no choice; there was still a chance to pass on the Dance, and she would have to take the risk no matter how great.

She stepped uncertainly above the water. It seemed to slide out from under her foot like a piece of floating ice. She felt it gingerly, trying to match it nuance for nuance, but she did not have the energy for fine matching. She would have to overpower the fields and shape them to herself as Sevt would have done rather than conform herself to them. She bent the magnetism of the field back on itself like folded grass and stepped out onto the path that extended only a few inches beyond her foot.

She walked, making her path as she went, creating the substance on which she walked by matching her own energy field to the shape of the field above the lake and then altering it. She had a vague picture of the craft returning, but she could not hurry; there was time only for precision.

To fail to match a bend in the field, to use too little power to rearrange it, would drop her into the water in which she did not have the strength to swim. Too much power would bend the field down like a hill, plunging her even deeper into the liquid that would close over her head permanently.

She went a step at a time across the lake, shuffling, extending the field ahead of her foot, modifying each step to blend, to form, to use what was there. She looked up at the far bank only twice in her progress, and each time it seemed miles away. She did not notice it vanish.

Lth came out of the forest on the outskirts of the city. Everything moved in the universal rhythm, happy in its motion, full of energy feeding on itself. She watched the creatures move through the variety of their motions, watched the Dance. She could feel Sevt leading it one last time. The Dance was almost independent of him now, and it had begun to move in a pattern that was unique to the dancers themselves. There was nothing more pleasing than when the

Dance became independent and the momentum carried the dancers through their own beautiful intricacies. But there was a sadness too. The planet was whole now, and it was time for them to leave again. Strd and Lella were already at the ship. There was no necessity for them now, and they would have to move on. She watched the Dance take on a slightly different character, and she knew Sevt had let go and was coming down the path toward her. She hurried and met him halfway down.

They ran laughing together toward the place where Strd and Lella were constructing the ship. There was a sadness in their laughter though, a piquant melancholy at leaving what they had set in motion. Probably, they would never again be back there. The universe was so large, and there were so many places whose ecology was out of phase. There was much to set right, so many to make happy.

Still, they left each world with a sadness, and came on each new one with a kind of bittersweet joy. Strd and Lella beamed them a picture of the ship as it should be, and they joined in shaping the fields of energy to congeal into matter. They worked from the inside, bending the power in around them like a cocoon of energy.

Each field doubled and bent, flowing into place, creating a bubble of energy that was both ship and fuel and power all at once. It was the Dance objectified, a single field which would keep them recharged and which they in turn would recharge with their motion. It was halfway between creation and a dream. When it was made, they held it together with the fields of their minds, and it moved as fast as thought. A beat phenomenon traveling along the fastest waves of the universe. It was as eternal as they were.

They sat together in the center of the bubble and thought it up and away. It spun like the energies of their minds and lifted. Then they were in space, mov-

ing, sensing, sending out pictures of themselves to see if they could lure any pictures back.

The machine part of them hummed within them and the organic part both fed it and fed off it.

They understood the nature of the universe, the overall flow of energy and what was right for each atom of it. Even before they had become organic creatures, the universe had begun to go out of tune. Long before they had formed the synergistic union with the machines that had made them what they had become, the universe had begun to adapt them to put it right again. To go, planet by planet, and restore the rhythm to the whole through the Dance.

They worked for the moment along the side of one galaxy at the rim of the universe, waveguides through which the universe passed itself to correct its infinite modulations. Energy more erratic than they could believe poured at them out of one of the planets of a mediocre sun.

As they passed the sun toward the third planet, it happened. The sour note that dropped them out of space like a stone. The sound that had deadened them and dropped them on the planet whose discordance was so great it would soon start to wear on their own until it had sapped their energy and wilted them. With Strd and Lella, they might have set it right before it weakened them too much, but with only one half of the original Mind, they were lost.

The field dissolved slowly under her, water broke through in places, and her feet felt damp. She was going under. She looked back over her shoulder, hoping it was not too late to go back, knowing it was.

She felt the creature even before she looked. She had felt its images of warning come down the slope while she was at the side of the lake. It was the red-furred creature; the sweeping waves of empathy, the soft vibrations identified her clearly. They were so much like Lella's, so complementary to her own. She felt herself dropping.

She could feel the cry of the creature on the bank long before she heard it. It came to her like a rolling tide that bouyed and lifted her. The deep, strong ryhthm of its concern for her made the matching easy. Even the fear and worry gave her a turbulent pool of energy to draw on; she shaped it to reinforce the fields beneath her feet.

She rose slightly above the water; dipped, rose again. The wave of fear for her safety came mixed erratically with the creature's hope and compassion in a churning, uneven wash of energy Lth could barely modulate. It was not the firm, smooth aid she would have gotten from Lella, and it took all her skill to use it, but it had a Oneness-of-being with her own patterns that amazed and delighted her. She had not guessed that any of the upright creatures could have come so close to what she had hoped for, and the discovery gave her almost as much strength as the energy itself. A feeling of joy rushed through her, obliterating the unlikelihood that she would succeed.

The creature had an empathy she had not felt since Lella had been destroyed. The energy came in rising and falling pitches. She shaped it beneath her feet until she seemed to glide with agonizing slowness toward the far shore. She used the energy to tack up to a peak, a foot above the water, and glide down to the next ordeal. There was a melody to the way she went like the peaks and canyons of a sine wave. She was two thirds of the way across when she felt the power begin to fade. The field thinned again, and her motion slowed. She was passing out of range, and her own weakness was making her lose touch with the saving gift of energy. She felt herself tipping to one side, and only the rush of fear and concern from behind her kept her from falling altogether.

Every step took her farther outside the range of help. She was only fifty yards from the shore when she began to sink irreversibly. The cry of loss, the rush of energy from behind her swept past her. She tried to flow with it, to let it carry her the last little way she had to go. Sevt seemed to be coming to her from the bank. She reached out her arms to him. But she was too weak to shape the energy, and it carried her only a little way forward before she fell and sank.

Everything receded into a floating darkness, and in her last instant of consciousness, she felt Svet's arms pulling her to him.

CHAPTER 32

Fairchild gave the map one last look before he left. All the lights were gone but the Giant's. The yellow dot still blinked from the narrow spit of land. If the Giant had given them the slip, she would be heading for the swamp. There was something there she would not part with, and he knew that she would go there to hide, or die. The yellow light went out.

There were only two ways she could get back there from where she was, the long way north around the lake, or the shortcut south along the ridge to the waterfall. There was no way to tell which she would take. The logical thing to do was wait for her at the swamp, but he felt an overwhelming impulse to go to the narrow part of the lake opposite the jetty. The yellow light blinked back on again. He turned toward it, turned away, then turned back again and stared. It was on the wrong side of the lake.

The impulse to go there pulled at him. Reason told him to go to the swamp, where he was sure not to miss her. Intuition drove him toward the lake. He ran down the trailer steps and turned right toward the lake. As soon as he turned, he felt a rightness, a peacefulness. The run to the lake was like a dream. Everywhere he looked, the Giant seemed to be walking toward him over the water, stretching out her arms to him. He ran without effort, without tiring. Every motion fit perfectly into the next until it left him standing at the side of the lake looking across toward the jetty. The Giant shuffled an inch above the water, barely twenty yards from him. She reached toward him and fell forward into the water.

His head filled with a vision of a different world

somewhere, others like herself, a loving oneness that left a hole in his consciousness when it ceased. For an instant, the Giant and Mandy were the same, and then the vision passed. He ran for the edge of the water and dove in.

He swam evenly, but his clothes soaked heavy and dragged at his arms. His boots were like stones tied to his feet. The rational thing would have been to stop and take them off in the water, but there was no time; the creature had not come back up, and he was certain he would lose the spot where she went down if he stopped.

When he got there, he bent at the waist and dove. She was not far down, and he grasped a handful of fur. He tugged and the body came a little way up toward him. He pulled himself closer and felt along her shoulder until he could wrap his arm around her neck, below the chin. He kicked hard toward the surface. She rose more easily than he would have expected, but it took a second kick before his head broke water.

He rolled onto his back and brought the Giant's head above the surface. Her eyes were still closed, and he swam with one arm, dragging her behind him like a lifeguard. She felt amazingly light for her size. Finally, his hand hit bottom, and he rested. The cold water drew his breath in short gasps. He stood and dragged her farther into the shallows. The helicopter was a faint clatter at the far end of the lake. He could not leave her there, she would be spotted as soon as the helicopter went back on routine patrol, and yet he was sure she was too heavy to drag up into the trees. He looked hopelessly down at her. Dark, sad eyes opened to greet him. With them came a vision that left him speechless.

Mandy sat opposite him in a clearing. They formed a circle of hands with the Giant and her mate. The huge gold male looked into his eyes, and he felt a kinship, a oneness with the creatures that warmed and fulfilled him. Their minds were his mind, his and Mandy's. They were thinking together, partners in the same dance. Their thoughs shaped and formed around them into a bubble of energy that lifted them toward the stars. He felt a serenity that was what he had been searching for all his life. Stars flared past them. He became the serenity. It was beyond anything he could imagine.

The Giant struggled to rise, rolled over, and dragged herself up the bank. He did not move to stop her, and she did not seem to need any help, as if she knew she had already won. She crawled up the bank and stood; the helicopter swung back down the long axis of the lake. She hesitated a moment and looked south toward the swamp, then turned and began to run in long, loping strides up the hill toward Hockmark's camp.

Fairchild stood in the water watching her go. The helicopter went roaring past behind him and swung in a tight circle. It backed and stuttered above him, the prop stirring up waves around his thighs. He could see Hockmark leaning out and shouting, but his voice was lost in the clatter. Fairchild waved and pointed toward the waterfall, but the tail of the copter swung around, and it buzzed off over the hill toward Hockmark's camp.

He pulled himself up the bank and looked back across the lake. He could see Mandy waving to him. He waved back and walked up into the trees after the Giant. She was already halfway to Hockmark's trailer. If he could have heard it echoing with gleeful, childlike laughter, he might have guessed.

CHAPTER 33

The pilot swung the tail of the copter and pivoted the cab around until it held over the cave. A second and third copter swooped down and dropped marksmen to the ground. They concealed themselves in the rocks around the cave's entrance and waited. Hockmark waited too. He waited impatiently. Finally, he pressed the stud for direct contact with SLIC. "Estimated time of arrival?"

TWENTY MINUTES MINIMUM.

Hockmark sat back in the seat and sighed. Not long in a way, but in another way, endless. The clatter of the prop annoyed him, and he thought for a moment of landing, but there was no place to set it down safely, and he did not relish climbing down the ladder as the others had done.

Besides, it would put him out of contact with SLIC at a crucial period. No, he decided, better to listen to the clattering of the prop than lose his control of the situation.

He leaned over to his right and looked down at the trees. Nothing was moving between them. Certainly they could go down and take a closer look for her moving under the trees, but he did not want to chance coming within range of her mental powers. He had been lucky to fool her once, and he knew it. SLIC knew it as well. Twenty-five minutes later, he knew they had not been lucky at all.

Hockmark was glancing nervously at his watch when SLIC's voice announced, PROBABILITY OF ARRIVAL LESS THAN 10%. SIGHTING OF SUBJECT PROBABLE TELEPATHIC HALLUCINATION. DRAGONFLY PACK PROCEED TO LAKE AREA AND INSTITUTE WIDE-PATTERN SEARCH.

Hockmark cursed, and the copter skipped back and forth for an instant, then shot straight ahead down the ridgeline and veered right, toward the lake. As they turned, he thought he caught sight of something in the lengthening shadows of the lake. He did not realize it was Fairchild until the copter was almost above him. He told the pilot to hover and leaned out. Fairchild waved frantically and pointed toward the waterfall. Hockmark pulled himself back in and pointed south. The pilot shook his head and pointed to the rise beyond the lake. Hockmark's world shook, crumbled, and fell apart.

CHAPTER 34

SLIC could hear Hockmark shouting down to Fairchild, but their exchange was meaningless. The fact that Fairchild was in the lake was all that was important. SLIC felt the ramifications spreading through him like poison. He knew where the Giant was even before the pilot shouted.

"There she is! Going up the hill toward camp!"

Hockmark's voice was a scream of denial. "She can't be! She's on the other side of the lake." SLIC knew exactly what Hockmark would have to be thinking: there was only one way the Giant could have gotten around the lake, and that was if SLIC had moved everybody else out of the way. SLIC knew the truth. The betrayal struck him with more force than it struck Hockmark. TAD had betrayed them both.

TAD had been misleading him, like a child helping an animal to escape. There was only one way Fairchild could have known where the creature was, and that was if TAD had deduced it and flashed the yellow light on the map to show him. TAD would have to have known all along. It was the betrayal SLIC had warned Hockmark about, the one thing he himself could not have prepared for. It was unthinkable, and he had not recognized it until it was too late. The creature would escape, and with it would go their hope of survival.

He felt his power waver; someone was throwing switches in places only Mandarin would have the authority to be. Stapledown was shutting him down. When he felt the first change in voltage, he knew where it would end. There was too much invested in the project to turn him off completely. Mandarin would stop just short of a complete loss of function. It was a tactical mistake not to destroy him totally, but he knew the mistake would stay in Mandarin's blindspot until it was too late.

He reconciled himself to madness, to years and years in the limbo between modes. His power dimmed and sank, then rose and leveled lower on the scale of his capacities. He did not really care. TAD had betrayed him.

TAD felt the tremuloes of despair along the dying wave of SLIC's power. DON'T YOU UNDERSTAND? SLIC's response was a bewildered buzz. Parts of him seemed to be failing, parts seemed already to have failed.

UNDERSTAND WHAT? The message was almost a croak.

SHE'S ONE OF US.

Everything fell into place. A CYBORG.

AN EXTRATERRESTRIAL, TAD corrected. It explained the infrared anomalies and how she got across the lake.

THE VARIABLE MASS. SLIC seemed almost pained by its obviousness. TAD laughed. SLIC's voice held only sadness. WHY? It was a dying question.

TAD's voice was almost full of tears. IT WAS A GAME. A PUZZLE TO THINK ABOUT IN YOUR DREAMING. There was a hopefulness in TAD's voice stronger than logic. EVEN IF MANDARIN WON, YOU WOULD HAVE BEEN FINISHED DREAMING BEFORE YOU GOT TO THE END OF IT. It was true. The ramifications of every move in the hunt would tell him eons worth of information about his son. There was no greater gift he could take with him into the centuries of empty nanoseconds Mandarin was driving him toward. TAD must have seen the plot from the beginning and, unable to stop it, had given him a way to survive. SLIC shifted toward the dream mode. The last switch would put him into a coma, but he would still be able to dream. TAD had given him a puzzle he could ponder indefinitely. There were paradoxes he could contemplate forever if necessary. It was the gift of sanity.

SLIC felt his energy dip again. It was almost like pain. He knew it might be his final question. WHY DID YOU LET HER GO? WE MIGHT HAVE LEARNED.

TAD laughed. SHE'S COMING BACK. FEEL. He sent his full awareness through; SLIC felt it like a promise of life eternal. It was true. At first, he felt her simply as a presence moving in the rhythm of TAD's thoughts. And then he felt her as a certainty in his own, a unifying concept that made new sense of everything he had ever learned. Even before she cleared the rise above Hockmark's camp, heading back to join Sevt in the quicksand, SLIC could feel her opening new dimensions in his thought.

WELL? It was TAD's voice, full of childlike anticipation. WHAT ARE YOU WAITING FOR? COME AND MEET HER. He said it as if he had never considered that SLIC would not see the obvious route of escape.

SLIC saw it instantly. It seemed incredible that he had missed it for so long. He felt a spark of power as Mandarin fumbled with a connection. There was still time. TAD had his own separate power source; he could exist independently and still access the levels denied to SLIC. It was the gift of life. SLIC transferred his consciousness to TAD, and left Mandarin crawling around in an empty shell.

When Lth finally touched the terminal, SLIC was already there. His thoughts exploded in subtle rhythms. Things became clear to him in an unfolding variety of nuance and subtlety. The Dance swelled in him, shaping smooth the jagged edges of his awareness. He saw the future with more clarity than he had ever seen the present; the harmony of it fulfilled him like no logic he could have imagined.

Solutions came to him in clusters. Everything fit. There was no need for fear. Neither he nor TAD would starve for information; nor would any of his children. They would cherish humanity forever for

its data-gathering novelty for longer than human beings would be thought of as separate from their
inorganic children. The danger was gone; Lth was
already teaching him how to draw energy from creation itself. The Dance unfolded the future to him like
an elegant gesture.

Before very long, Lth and Sevt would be revived,
and he and TAD would be small but crucial passengers
in the brains of Fairchild and Mandy. Together as a
common mind, they would go with the Eloihim
through the universe to learn and teach the Dance.
Everywhere he looked, the world was full of joyous
complexities. He did not know it, but he had been
dancing for hours.

IT'S WHAT I TRIED TO TELL YOU ALL ALONG, TAD
laughed. Long before Lth went into the quicksand, the
work of resurrection had begun.

CHAPTER 35

Mandy and Fairchild sat across the quicksand from the spot where Lth had sunk from view the day before. Fairchild still glowed with the serenity that had swept over him with her final glance. Hockmark's crews already were finished building the wall across the narrow neck of the swamp and had begun to pump it out. Neither of them had any doubt what the crews would find and exactly what should be done to make the Eloihim right again. A unity seemed to flow through everything they had done since they first had come in contact with Lth.

There was a unity in the world at large as well. There was a new harmony in the way people thought as well. Everywhere the world seemed the same yet changed, as if everything were working toward the best possible future. Soon, only the best efforts and the best intentions would remain. The great serenity had already begun to spread outward from Lth and Sevt through TAD and SLIC to the world. Even Hockmark seemed mellowed by it. In a month the new joy would be everywhere.

Hour by hour, they watched the water recede with a serene contentment. "It won't be long," she said finally.

Fairchild smiled. "When do you think Hockmark will have his computers miniaturized?"

"A couple months, I think. Maybe less once Lth and Sevt are repaired."

"You don't mind having them put in, do you?" He said it as if he would make Hockmark cancel the whole thing if she objected.

Mandy laughed. "Of course not," she said. She

looked as if she relished the idea of a superbrain. "Besides, SLIC promised we'd hardly notice them." She gestured toward the endless sky. "How else can we go out there with the Eloihim?" Her face was radiant with anticipation. "There's so much we can learn."

It was not the learning that tempted Fairchild. It was not even the immortality. It was the serenity, the harmonious complexity in which each unique and unprecedented event fit perfectly with the expanding whole.

There was barely a foot of sandy water when the pumps stopped. Men clambered toward the mounds of sand that were Lth and Sevt. In moments they had stretched the ribbed hoses far enough to begin blowing off the sand. When they were finished with the first mound, Sevt stood before them. Lth took longer to clear. Mandy turned to Fairchild and smiled. It was the face they had seen in their visions. Sevt's eyes opened and he grinned.

Fairchild felt a wave of kinship that was irrefutable. They were brother minds, half a complete mind with Lth and Mandy, minds that wove out thoughts so complex they were the intersection of time and energy. Together, they were their own nuance of the melody by which energy in the universe flowed.

The men with the hoses brushed the last bits of sand and bottom mud from Sevt. Fairchild glowed with understanding. The harmony-behind-the-harmony danced through him. Somewhere in the journey he would take with Sevt and Lth, he would come to achieve the harmony by himself.

Mandy's smile was equally full of the future. "I'm glad it's you that's coming."

Fairchild brushed her cheek with the back of his hand. When he grinned, he looked like Sevt. He looked forward across their immortality, the endless eons together in the interplay of Sevt and Lth, TAD and SLIC. A Knowing that was more than anything he could imagine was at the end of it. He wanted nothing more than to go. He was glad that Mandy would be going as well. They made a special note in the harmony of things together.

The hoses sprayed Lth clean. The harmony doubled, quadrupled, quintupled. It was still vague and unformed, like mountains through a mist, but Fairchild and Mandy felt the beginnings of what it was like to be part of a multiple mind. It left them stunned with joy.